Play for Love

Helena Stone

Copyright

Acknowledgements

I couldn't have written this story if it hadn't been for a wealth of amazing childhood memories. Reshaping my former summer home and playground so it is perfect for Seb and Rutger without losing the community spirit and activities I remember so fondly has been delightful.

I can't thank K Evan Coles, Sherry Mahnken, and Paul Wright enough for being the best beta readers in the world. As always, Tanja Ongkiehong's editing and proof reading skills make me look much better than I actually am.

Massive thanks also to Brigham Vaughn for the gorgeous cover design.

Dedication

This book is dedicated to Landgoed De Leperkoen in Lunteren, The Netherlands and a childhood worth of very fond memories.

Chapter One

Landed.

Seb sent off the text as he watched his fellow passengers on the plane scramble to get up, retrieve their luggage, and throw impatient glances at the doors, which remained closed for the moment. He'd never understood that rush. He had no idea why people stood up in a space that wasn't high enough for them to stretch. Sure, the seats weren't comfortable, but as far as Seb was concerned, it sure beat the kink he would get in his neck if he stood.

His phone dinged, and Seb glanced at the screen.

Ready for you in arrivals. Can't wait to see you.

Not much longer. If they ever open the doors ☹

Seb hit Send and focused on the impatient crowd surrounding him. Being irritated about their irrational behavior was more comfortable than dealing with the nerves swirling in his belly. In a matter of minutes, he'd meet his hero. That fact on its own was enough to make his blood flow faster. Since his hero was also the most attractive man Seb had ever laid eyes on, it was a minor miracle Seb could still think straight.

"Ladies and gentlemen, we apologize for the delay. The ground crew informed me there are some issues with the stairs, so it will be a little longer before we can open the doors. Please remain seated."

The pilot's announcement was greeted by a few curses and many frustrated faces from the other passengers. Seb limited himself to a resigned sigh and messaged Rutger to let him know about the delay. Since he was in the right app anyway and had time to kill, Seb scrolled back over the messages he and Rutger had exchanged over the past six months, ever since they'd found themselves fighting for the same side during a Twitter shitstorm.

A smile teased his lips as he read those early texts. They'd been so polite and courteous with each other. At first, their chats had centered on video games, and Seb had marveled as it became clear how closely their tastes in games matched. His wonder had turned into awe when he'd figured out who Rutger was. He still couldn't quite believe that the game designer Seb had admired ever since he'd first played *Raeynar's Realm* was chatting with him and didn't show any sign of wanting their conversations to end.

He arrived at the part of the conversation where they'd

discovered they were both gay. They'd been chatting for over a month by then. That had been when the flirting had started, first via text but quickly followed by video calls. Virtual sex had been a recent development, and those sessions went a long way toward explaining why Seb now found himself on a plane in Schiphol Airport. For half a second, Seb was tempted to open one of the videos and watch Rutger as he brought himself to an orgasm. Common sense immediately kicked in, and Seb pushed his phone into his pocket. He could imagine all too well how the friendly elderly lady sitting next to him might react if she got an eyeful of Rutger while he gave himself a hand job.

Movement at the front of the plane caught Seb's attention, and he looked up hopefully. He would only be in the Netherlands for about thirty-six hours. Every minute stuck on this damned plane meant a minute less with Rutger.

The cabin crew opened the door, and as if they'd fired a starting pistol, all but a few of the passengers got to their feet again. Seb remained seated, just as he'd done the first time, as thoughts continued to swirl through his head.

What am I doing here?

He knew the answer to that question. He'd come because he couldn't wait to meet Rutger face-to-face. Because he needed to know whether or not the attraction between them would survive in-person contact. Despite chatting regularly for six months, there was still so much about Rutger he didn't know, and Seb couldn't wait to learn more. First and foremost, though, he'd traveled because every cell in Seb's body longed to feel Rutger's lips against his, Rutger's skin beneath his fingers, Rutger's cock in his mouth and… Seb knew why he'd made the journey; he just hated that he couldn't stay longer. Thirty-six hours wasn't enough to—

"Could you give me a hand, pet?" The grey-haired woman sitting next to him gave Seb a hopeful smile. "The flight attendant put my suitcase in the locker for me, but he appears to be busy now."

"Of course." Most of their fellow passengers had already made their way off the plane, so as soon as the lady stepped into the narrow aisle, Seb got to his feet and pulled her bright purple suitcase from the overhead locker. He blinked. He'd expected something more traditional or old-fashioned for someone her age. He gave himself a mental kick. Stereotypes seldom reflected reality.

"Thank you. You're a good lad." She patted Seb's upper arm before heading for the exit, pulling her bright case along behind her.

A good lad. How long had it been since anyone had said that about him? At least fifteen years, Seb guessed. His mother had never used pet words, so it would have been his granny who last addressed him like that, and she had died when Seb was ten.

He extracted his overnight bag from beneath the chair in front of his, then walked to the exit of the now empty plane. Waiting a while always paid off, and he couldn't believe more people hadn't come to the same conclusion.

As he made his way through the airport, Seb's thoughts returned to Rutger. They had met on Twitter after they'd both posted the same reply in response to a ludicrous statement about gaming. He couldn't remember the exact wording of the instigating tweet, but the reaction both he and Rutger had given was etched into his mind. *What does it say about you if you can't get past level 2 of a game you call childish?*

That had set the original poster and a surprising number of trolls off. Initially, Seb had enjoyed the discussion, but it hadn't been long before it devolved into the usual cascade of verbal abuse. Seb had been about to sign off when he'd received a direct message from Rutger.

Seb glared at the long lines of people waiting to have their passports checked by machines that appeared to be operating in slow motion. *Just my luck.* He picked a queue and said a silent prayer that for once, he would be lucky, and it wouldn't turn out to be the most sluggish line.

As he shuffled closer to his destination, Seb's thoughts returned to that Twitter meeting with Rutger. Rather than logging off early, he'd stayed up well past his usual sensible bedtime while he chatted with Rutger about computer games. It had been a revelation to connect with someone who enjoyed the same games Seb loved and mostly for the same reasons. His first impression had been that Rutger understood the ins and outs of gaming at least as well as Seb did. It had been an ultimate nerdfest, and Seb hadn't thought twice before he'd reached out to Rutger again the following evening.

After what felt like a lifetime, the passport machine took, inspected, and returned Seb's passport and allowed him to enter the luggage reclaim area. Since he'd carried everything he'd brought in his holdall, Seb strode past it and into the arrivals hall.

Wow.

Amsterdam airport dwarfed its Dublin equivalent. That had been true for the long trek from his gate to where Seb was now, and it was even more obvious here. At first glance, Seb spotted bars, restaurants, and a wide variety of shops, as well as signs pointing to the usual car rental places and foreign exchange counters.

"Sebastian, you're here." A deep, resonant voice pulled Seb from his observations.

"So I am." Whatever else he might have said fled Seb's mind as he focused on the man who'd addressed him, and discovered he had to tilt his head back a little to meet Rutger's gaze. *Holy fuck.* He'd known what to expect thanks to their numerous video calls. But nothing had prepared him for Rutger's sheer in-person hotness or the breathtaking aura of strength and calm he radiated. Rutger's short, dark blond hair stood up from his head. His full beard and mustache were the same color as his hair, interspersed with lighter specks. His blue eyes were bright, and small laughter lines crinkled at their sides. Seb imagined what it might be like to thread his fingers through that beard or to feel the scrape of the stubble on the side of Rutger's head, where the hair had been shaved. Seb didn't break out of his trance until Ruther lifted his eyebrows at him. "And you must be Rutger."

"That's me," Rutger confirmed, sounding amused.

Way to go, Seb. Mere seconds after meeting Rutger, Seb had already managed to make a fool of himself. The almost fifteen years between them had never been an issue while they chatted—and engaged in other activities—online. Seb wasn't sure how long that would remain true if he didn't stop acting like a lovestruck teenager.

Seconds ticked by while they stood there, taking each other in. Seb's blood heated as Rutger's gaze traveled from the top of his head to his feet. Not wanting to be left behind, Seb forced his eyes away from Rutger's face and inspected the rest of him. He drank in the broad shoulders and was grateful Rutger wasn't wearing a coat so he could appreciate his slim waist and powerful legs too.

There was no doubt about it. Rutger was every one of Seb's fantasies come to life…and then some.

"Ugh" Somebody walked into Seb or pushed him, and he found himself propelled forward and almost losing his balance.

"Careful." Rutger grabbed Seb's upper arms and steadied him. "Are you okay?" The laughter on Rutger's face had been replaced by concern.

For a fleeting moment, Seb thought Rutger might kiss him right there, in the middle of Schiphol Airport. Then Rutger pulled him into a half hug that was both awkward and amazing at the same time. When Rutger released him, it was all Seb could do not to cling to him.

"We should probably move. I think we're in the way here." Rutger's voice held a rough edge that suggested the embrace hadn't left him unaffected either.

"Sounds like a plan." Seb hoped that moving would give him the opportunity to gather himself. He wouldn't be around for long enough to make a bad first impression and hope to fix the situation too. He had to get this right from the start.

"Do you want to eat or drink something first?" Rutger

asked as he led the way through the crowds and past the various outlets. "It takes about an hour to get to my place, so…"

"I'm good. I had coffee and a bite to eat before I got on the plane, and the flight only takes about an hour." What was more, Seb couldn't imagine yearning for food as much as he longed to be alone with Rutger. An hour was longer than he wanted to wait before he could touch Rutger and taste him. He'd rather starve than put more time between now and the moment he would get what he'd been hungering for ever since Rutger had invited him.

"Great." The gleam in Rutger's eyes indicated that he might be on the same page as Seb.

Seb followed Rutger into the parking lot and to a blue Mitsubishi Outlander.

"Nice," Seb muttered.

"It's nothing fancy," Rutger said as he unlocked the doors with his key fob. "But it gets me from A to B, and it's sturdy, which is probably for the best, considering where I live." He chuckled, and the sound was warm and comforting. "A fancy car wouldn't last long there."

"Looks okay to me." Although Seb knew how to drive, he had never bothered getting a car. He lived and worked in Dublin. His parents were a twenty-minute bus drive away from the rental apartment he shared with two other men. Most of the time he had no need for a car, and he rarely wished he owned one.

After he'd dumped his holdall on the back seat, Seb reached for the handle of the front car door, only to connect with Rutger's fingers.

"Are you driving?" Rutger smirked.

"What?" Seb turned his head and saw the steering wheel. "Right." He mentally slapped his forehead. "I forgot that you lot drive on the wrong side of the road." He stepped back and walked around the car.

"The right side you mean," Rutger said as soon as they were both inside the car. "I mean, it's obvious, isn't it? We even drive on the *right* side of the road."

"Sure," Seb said, enjoying himself. "But our steering wheels are on the *right* side." He turned to his left and grinned at Rutger. The exchange felt familiar. Their online interactions had been like this. Fast. Fun. With both of them always trying to outsmart the other. And Rutger usually winning.

Seb zoomed in on Rutger and drank in the details as if he'd never seen him before. He leaned forward, lowering his gaze to Rutger's lips, imagining the moment he would taste them for the first time.

Rutger moved his head, put the car in reverse, and pulled out of his parking spot.

No kiss? Seb turned his head and inspected the parking area around them. He didn't see a living soul. He could understand Rutger being uncomfortable about public displays of intimacy; Seb wasn't a huge fan either. But there was no public to see them. *I'm only here for thirty-six hours. Now's not the time to play coy.*

"As tempting as you are," Rutger said while he maneuvered them through very narrow passages and ramps to the exit, "I'm not sure I could make myself stop if I kissed you now."

Seb's disappointment melted away, and his blood heated. He'd known the attraction between them was strong and mutual before he made his journey. To have it confirmed now—to know that Rutger wanted him as much as Seb wanted Rutger—was a relief and delighted him.

Traffic outside the building was chaotic. Seb was sure at least part of the issue was that cars appeared to be coming at him from the wrong direction, but between busses, taxis, cars, bicycles, and pedestrians, Seb was very happy he wasn't driving. Since he imagined Rutger needed to concentrate to safely get them away from the airport, Seb kept silent.

A short while later, Rutger pulled into a lane on the highway. "So." He threw Seb a glance before focusing on the road again. "Your journey was okay?"

"Sure." Seb shrugged. "Considering I had to get up at stupid o'clock in the morning to get to the airport on time, it wasn't too bad."

"How early is stupid o'clock exactly?" Rutger sounded amused.

"Three."

"Ouch. You must be exhausted." Rutger's amusement turned into concern, and a frown appeared on his forehead.

"It's not that bad." Seb didn't want Rutger to think he was tired. "Besides, taking the next flight would have meant losing most of today. My visit is short enough as it is." Seb couldn't prevent the bitter note from creeping into his voice.

"You're upset about that?" Rutger asked.

"I wouldn't have minded staying longer," Seb said, unsure how to interpret Rutger's question. Did Rutger mean that a day and a half was long enough for him? Or was he just curious about Seb's state of mind? "What I'm upset about is that my bastard of a boss refused to give me more time off. I only took seven days of my allotted annual leave this year. I asked him for one week. One week! And he told me no."

"Why?" Rutger asked. "I mean, he must have given you a reason."

"Because he's a bollix." Seb sighed. "Because he claims we're too close to finalizing the campaign I'm involved with. He says he wants all hands on deck for the time being."

"That doesn't sound unreasonable?" Rutger spoke slowly as if he was afraid he might be saying the wrong thing.

"It isn't," Seb agreed. "And it would have been okay if it hadn't been for the fact that he's been on leave since before Christmas. We haven't seen him. But he did phone in every day to make sure all of his underlings were present and accounted for." Seb pushed out a fake laugh. "In the end, he allowed me to take today. With tomorrow being a bank holiday, that means I'm all yours for the next thirty"—he thought for a moment; time was ticking away—"five or so hours."

"Well. It's better than nothing." The cheer in Rutger's voice held a distinct note of resignation.

"True that." Seb leaned back, relaxing against the headrest, and closed his eyes, just for a moment. Getting up at three had not been a hardship. He'd been excited about his trip, eager to get going, and impatient about meeting Rutger.

A song, sung in a language Seb didn't understand, filtered through his thoughts, and he assumed Rutger had turned on the sound system. The music, especially the lyrics, intrigued Seb. He had no idea what any of it meant, but the song felt filled with emotion, almost sad yet soothing at the same time.

The music changed to something classical and peaceful. Seb thought about opening his eyes, but his eyelids felt too heavy. He couldn't focus on his thoughts anymore either and allowed them to float along with the music. He was here. He'd made it to the Netherlands. He was in a car with Rutger, on his way to Rutger's house and the fulfillment of everything he'd dreamed about for the past four weeks.

Are we there ye…

Chapter Two

Rutger almost laughed out loud when a soft snore escaped Seb. For someone who'd claimed not to be exhausted only minutes ago, he'd sure managed to doze off with great ease. He bit the inside of his cheek to stop himself from making any sound that might disturb Seb and focused on the road. Thankfully, it wasn't too busy. Any other time of the year, he would have been caught up in the last of the morning rush hour traffic, but given that it was New Year's Eve, the drive home would be smooth and uninterrupted.

He glanced at Seb. Asleep, he looked younger than his twenty-six years, and Rutger wondered if he should be concerned about how much that observation thrilled him. Seb's skin was smooth, as if he'd taken the time to shave before traveling or didn't need to deal with facial hair all that often. The heavy black eyebrows should have given his face a somber demeanor but instead highlighted Seb's fair skin and rosy lips.

Rutger signaled and overtook a truck as his thoughts lingered on Seb's mouth. He wasn't sure where he'd found the strength to turn away from what had clearly been an invitation to kiss. Knowing that it had been the right thing to do, that they would probably still be in that parking lot if he hadn't, didn't make him regret the decision any less. Ever since they'd first started chatting online and even before he'd known Seb was gay too, there'd been something about Seb that had made Rutger's blood flow faster.

Said blood took that moment to head for Rutger's groin. Unless he could divert his thoughts, the rest of his journey might end up distinctly uncomfortable. *Radar Love* by Golden Earring started on the radio, and Rutger mouthed the words along with Barry Hay. Singing out loud would have been better, but he didn't want to wake the Sleeping Beauty beside him.

"We're here." He nudged Seb's shoulder.

"Wha?" Seb blinked a few times before squinting at his surroundings. "Wow. You weren't joking when you said you lived in the middle of nowhere."

"Did you think I was?" Rutger took in the trees and bushes enclosing the small clearing in front of his cabin and tried to see the place he called home through Seb's eyes.

Seb shrugged. "Not really. It's just that the middle of nowhere is such a vague term. Some of my friends swear high and low that the Dublin suburbs fall into that category."

Rutger laughed. "I'm sorry. The closest town is more than ten minutes away. If you were hoping for pubs and clubs…" He deliberately left the rest of his sentence hanging as he opened his door and got out of the car. What if pubs and clubs were exactly what Seb had been hoping for?

As soon as Seb stood next to the car, he lifted his hands over his head and stretched, with his face turned to the sky.

Rutger drank in the slim outline of Seb, the stretch of his upper body, his long legs, and his very well-formed and extremely squeezable arse. He'd fantasized about all the things he would do once he got his hands on Seb so often that it was hard to believe he was minutes away from making those dreams reality.

"Do you have neighbors?" Seb turned on his spot as he inspected the surrounding forest.

"I do." Rutger rounded the car and stepped up behind Seb. "Look." Over Seb's shoulder, he pointed to a lane leading away from them. "There's another cabin there." He grabbed Seb's shoulders and softly turned him to the left. "And over there too. Can you see them?"

"Just about. If you hadn't pointed them out, I would have missed them."

Rutger chuckled. "That's the idea. In summer, when everything is green, it is easy to forget I have other people living not too far away."

"And you don't mind? You don't get lonely?" Seb

turned until he faced Rutger again without dislodging Rutger's hands from his shoulders.

The various answers Rutger might have given slipped his mind as he looked into Seb's bright blue eyes. He'd waited long enough. "I'm glad you're here." He bowed his neck and pressed his lips against Seb's. "Very glad." He cupped the back of Seb's head and raked his fingers through the soft black hair as he claimed Seb's mouth, his impatience making him more forceful than he'd intended.

Seb didn't seem to mind. If anything, he appeared to thrive on it. He grabbed the front of Rutger's woolen top with both hands and surrendered to the demands of Rutger's mouth. The moment Rutger prodded with his tongue, Seb opened up for him and welcomed the intrusion with a soft, inarticulate sound. It was everything Rutger had hoped for and so much more. For once, his imagination didn't compare to the magic of reality. Or maybe this was the first time he'd met a man who was a match for the illusions his mind conjured up.

The world faded away as Rutger took his fill from Seb's mouth. Their tongues danced, teased, enticed. Teeth nibbling on his lip heated Rutger's blood. The soft but insistent sounds falling from Seb's lips fed Rutger's hunger. Desperate for more, Rutger snuck his hand under Seb's jacket, and he continued to peel at Seb's clothes until his fingers connected with a strip of naked skin.

A violent shiver ran through Seb and broke the spell. "Fuck. That's cold."

"Sorry." Rutger pulled his hand back and wanted to slap himself with it. What was wrong with him? The temperature was near freezing. He had a perfectly good and warm house a few steps away. "Come." He took Seb's hand. "We'll have you warmed up in no time."

Seb's laughter rang out as he retrieved his bag from the car and allowed himself to be pulled along. "The only cool part of my body is where you touched my skin. The rest is running hot. Trust me."

Rutger bit back his own laugh so his hand was steady when he pushed the key into the lock. He didn't want to wait another minute. The moment he opened the door, a flash of black and white, barking excitedly, flashed by them.

"Raeynar! Come here."

"Raeynar?" Seb followed the dog with his gaze as it ran to the trees. "I thought his name was Ray. Did you call him after your game?"

"Quite the opposite. Raey is five years old. I got him soon after I moved here."

The border collie lifted his leg against a tree before turning around and trotting back to the house.

"Bad boy," Rutger said when his dog jumped up against him.

"Aren't you supposed to sound as if you mean it when you're telling your dog off?" Seb's amusement was obvious. "He's gorgeous." Seb held out his hand so Raeynar could smell it. "Just like his—" A blush erupted on Seb's face as he knelt to pet the dog who was taking an obvious and enthusiastic interest in the guest his owner had brought home if the speed with which he wagged his tail was any indication. Since Raey normally took his time before getting friendly with strangers, Rutger took it as a positive sign.

As tempting as it was to ask Seb to finish his sentence, Rutger refrained. The last thing he wanted to do right now was to make Seb uncomfortable. Besides, he could guess what the missing word was, and it delighted him. He knew he wasn't bad looking, but he had worried that the age difference between them might become too obvious once they were face-to-face. Then again, maybe Seb had a thing for older men to match Rutger's preference for those who were younger than he was.

"That's enough, Raey. Get in."

The canine in question gave Rutger a reproaching look before obeying the order. As soon as Seb had straightened, Rutger took his hand and pulled him into the house, eager to get to his bedroom and at last indulge in everything he'd fantasized about since Seb had announced his visit.

As they moved through the front porch into the open-plan living area, Seb slowed down. The temptation to just keep going at full speed and drag Seb with him was great, but Rutger resisted. He had no intention of interrupting their journey to the bedroom, but he could allow Seb a moment or two to get a first glimpse at the interior.

As soon as he stepped into his bedroom, the smell of lavender-scented washing powder hit Rutger's nose. He'd changed the sheets before he'd left for the airport earlier as part of a determined effort to ensure everything was as perfect as he could make it.

When they arrived at the foot of his bed, Rutger halted and turned to Seb.

"Well, now." Seb's smirk had a touch of uncertainty to it. "I would almost think you're happy to see me."

"You have no idea." The words escaped Rutger without forethought, and he saw the surprise on Seb's face. "Am I moving too fast?" He wanted Seb with an urgency that bordered on desperation, but he would wait—with great difficulty—if he had to.

"No." Seb shook his head as if to emphasize his answer." He reached for Rutger and unwound his scarf.

A combination of relief and lust flowed through

Rutger's veins, making his fingers clumsy when he unbuttoned Seb's coat and removed it.

They didn't rush undressing each other, but they didn't linger either. Items of clothing fell to the floor in a steady rhythm. It wasn't until they'd worked their way through the layers of winter wear and reached naked skin that their pace slowed.

Rutger traced a hand from Seb's hip to his shoulder, keeping his touch light while his eyes drank in the expanse of creamy-white skin, the faint outline of abs on Seb's stomach, and his tempting nipples. Unable to deny himself, Rutger bent forward and took one of the little buds between his lips. He teased with his tongue and carefully used his teeth until Seb's breathing became loud and faster. Rutger's erection pushed hard against his fly, and he was caught between the urge to let loose and throw caution to the wind and the desire to take his time to explore Seb. They had less than thirty-six hours. God only knew when he might get to do this again, but in the meantime, he wanted to explore every inch of Seb's body and commit it to memory.

"Fuck." Seb sighed the word. "You're driving me insane. Let me see all of you."

"Your wish…" Rutger grinned as he released Seb and took a step back, immediately reaching for the button on his jeans. He refrained from opening it when he noticed that Seb hadn't moved. Instead, he appeared frozen, with his gaze fixed on Rutger's stomach or—and that option was far more probable— on his treasure trail. "Am I getting naked on my own?"

Seb shook his head and raised his gaze. "No. It's just…" He waved his hand at Rutger's torso. "So little time. So much man."

"All the more reason to get a move on," Rutger said with a smile. "Time's a-wasting." The obvious admiration and desire in Seb's eyes boosted his confidence no end. He opened his jeans and pushed them and his boxer shorts down without taking his eyes off Seb, who did the same. His mouth watered when Seb's cock bounced a little upon release. It was long and slim and oh-so tempting.

"Oh." Seb sucked in air through his teeth, creating a hissing sound. "You're gorgeous." The breathless quality of Seb's voice was gratifying and stoked the fire raging through Rutger a bit higher. "All of you."

It was strange, funny even. They'd seen each other naked before. But the screen had not been able to convey the glorious beauty of Seb's body, the glow of his skin, or the fire in his eyes.

"Real-life you is so much better," Seb muttered,

echoing Rutger's thoughts.

They stood there with less than a meter separating them, for goodness only knew how long. Rutger had no idea what was going on in Seb's head, but if he was on the same page as Rutger, Seb was committing everything he saw to memory. The picture now, soon to be followed by touch and taste.

Suddenly, looking wasn't enough anymore, and Rutger launched himself at Seb. He grabbed Seb around his middle and tumbled both of them to the bed, where they bounced as they landed.

"Hey." Seb laughed. "You only had to ask."

Rutger was done with words; he had better uses for his mouth. He pushed Seb onto his back and draped himself over him. Seb's mouth was right there, so he claimed it. He redistributed his weight a little until his cock pressed against Seb's soft belly and Seb's rock-hard dick rested against Rutger's upper thigh.

After only a few kisses, Rutger found himself addicted to the taste of Seb. He couldn't get enough of the feel of his tongue as it alternately battled with Rutger's and caressed it. Soft sounds fell from Seb's lips, feeding the hunger in Rutger. He undulated, already resigned to the fact that this first encounter would be over before it had properly started. He just didn't have the patience; his need ran too high. Weeks of anticipating this moment, combined with the reality of it far outstripping his imagination, meant his restraint was shot.

Seb moved with him, pushing his body closer against Rutger's for more friction while his almost black eyes were locked on Rutger's. It was so easy to imagine fires burning behind those dilated pupils, a raging furnace like the one roaring inside Rutger.

"Wanted this so badly," Seb mumbled.

"Me too." Rutger wasn't sure Seb knew what he'd just said, but he agreed.

Seb grabbed the back of Rutger's head with both hands and tangled his fingers into Rutger's hair. At the same time, he arched up and rutted harder against Rutger. Rutger moved with Seb, relishing each slide of his cock across Seb's soft tummy, already slick with precum.

"Yes." Seb breathed the word as he stiffened against Rutger. "Oh, yes."

The combination of Seb's dick pulsing against his thigh and the smell of Seb's orgasm hitting his nose was enough to send Rutger over too. "Fuck." His orgasm claimed his body. Muscles stiffened and relaxed, lights flashed before his eyes, and his release seemed endless, as though he had been saving it for this moment.

His strength failed him the moment his orgasm finished,

as if his muscles and bones had been liquified. Thankfully, Rutger's brain remained functional a little longer, and he managed to drop to the covers next to Seb rather than collapse on top of him. As soon as he hit the bed, he reached for Seb and pulled him close. Seb turned his head and gave him a sweet, bliss-filled smile.

"That was…I don't know. Spectacular."

Rutger returned the smile. "It was, wasn't it?" He pressed his lips against Seb's forehead. Having Seb in his bed felt good, as if he belonged there, and Rutger had to remind himself it would only be for one night. Seb had been right when he'd called his boss a bastard for not allowing him more time off. "We should probably get up," Rutger suggested.

"Not yet," Seb muttered. "I'm too comfortable."

The statement sent a thrill of satisfaction through Rutger. He didn't really want to get up either, so he grabbed the wet wipes he kept next to his bed and gave both of them a cursory cleanup.

Taking a few minutes to simply enjoy holding each other was perfect. He didn't know if the same was true for Seb, but one of Rutger's most persistent fantasies had been of having Seb in his arms, keeping him close. As much as they only had a limited amount of time, he didn't want to rush this part of their coming together. He tightened his hold on Seb and watched as

Seb's eyes fluttered closed.

Yes, they could afford to take a moment or two before they got busy again. Rutger already knew this would be one of his favorite memories of these two days.

Chapter Three

When he first emerged from his slumber and before he opened his eyes, Seb only knew the mattress beneath him was firmer than the one he was used to. He couldn't remember the last time he'd woken up beside someone else either. Then his brain kicked in. *Rutger.* Seb was in the Netherlands. He'd at last met the man who'd occupied his mind for the past few months, face-to-face. They'd enjoyed—except that enjoyed wasn't a strong enough word—a wild and uncoordinated bout of sex that had all but blown his mind.

A delighted shudder coursed through his body. Seb opened his eyes and discovered his nose was mere inches away from Rutger's. His host was asleep, and Seb took the time to stare at him without feeling shy about it. He'd known Rutger was gorgeous, of course. They'd spent enough time video calling each other that Rutger's face was now almost as familiar to Seb as his own. Close up and personal was immeasurably better, though, and Seb drank Rutger's features in, committing every detail to memory so he would be able to call them up at will when he was back in Dublin…on his own again.

There was nothing about Rutger for Seb to find fault with. Quite the opposite, in fact. As far as Seb was concerned,

Rutger was as close to perfect as it was possible for any mortal man to be. The thick blond hair, now standing up in random tuffs, with the lower parts shaved to a stubble around his ears and neck, made Seb's fingers itch to touch. He wanted to feel that stubble against his hand once more, comb Rutger's beard with his fingers. He couldn't wait to feel those lips against his again and on other parts of his body.

Seb turned his head and realized for the first time that they'd dozed off without pulling the covers over themselves first. And he wasn't cold despite the temperature outside having been low enough for his breath to be visible. He was impressed. When he'd first spotted the cabin, he'd assumed it would be a cold, possibly drafty, and damp place. Not that the house looked old or decrepit; far from it. It was more that it had seemed to belong in the forest as if it had earned its spot amidst the trees.

He bit back a chuckle, afraid he'd wake Rutger if he made a noise. Not that Seb had any intention of letting him sleep for long. Their time together was short and precious, and right now, it was a-wasting. But a tired and/or grumpy Rutger wouldn't be fun either, so allowing him a bit more shut-eye was probably the best option. Besides, it was New Year's Eve. Chances were their evening and night would be long and, if Seb had anything to say about it, memorable.

Slowly, making sure to disturb the mattress as little as

possible, Seb rolled himself to the side of the bed and got up. He wanted to satisfy his curiosity about the rest of Rutger's house. He'd barely noticed the interior while they made their way to the bedroom, and he was going to make up for that now. If Rutger was still sleeping when Seb finished his exploration, he'd wake him up then. Seb could think of a few fun ways to rouse his host.

He spotted his shirt on the floor and put it on, although he wasn't sure why. Since they were alone and Rutger had no neighbors in sight of the house, there was no need for modesty.

Outside the bedroom, Seb turned right, to the part of the house he hadn't been in yet, and two steps later, he found himself in a small but well-designed kitchen. He'd also gained company. Raeynar sat next to Seb, looking up at him with his tongue lolling. Seb scratched him between his ears while he took in the gas cooker, the relatively large fridge-freezer, and the collection of pots and pans hanging from a rack over the counter. It was something they'd never talked about, but it seemed that Rutger probably enjoyed cooking.

As if the observation had given it a reminder, Seb's stomach rumbled. One glance at the digital display on the microwave explained the sound. It was almost one o'clock. He heaved a sigh of relief. Apparently, they hadn't slept the day away. Still, given that Seb had eaten breakfast at six that morning, it was hardly surprising he was hungry. He resisted the temptation to search the fridge for a quick snack and returned to his investigation of Rutger's world.

Ignoring both Rutger's bedroom and the closed door opposite it, Seb walked to the front of the house, Raeynar keeping him company. He'd barely seen the porch or the living room when they'd arrived. He smiled. Rutger had been in such a hurry to get him to the bedroom. Then again, he'd been just as eager. Their earlier rush meant that he hadn't noticed the beautiful, possibly handcrafted, wooden table that stood in front of the large windows that overlooked the forest and the small clearing where Rutger had parked his car. In some of the trees next to the house, he saw what looked like small tables that served as bird feeders. A movement caught his eye, and he adjusted his assessment. Obviously, these were squirrel feeders. He smiled as two red rodents with beautiful, bushy tails helped themselves to whatever food had been placed there for them. Red squirrels were few and far between in Ireland, and he allowed himself a little time to enjoy the sight of them.

His stomach made another plaintive sound, and Seb turned and faced the rest of the house. It was almost time to wake Rutger up, and not just because Seb was hungry. Twenty-four hours from now, they would be on the road again to get Seb to the airport on time. Sleeping should be kept to an absolute minimum.

He liked the living room with its beige, L-shaped couch. Red patterned cushions brightened what might otherwise have been a rather boring piece of furniture. A large screen was mounted on the wall opposite the seating corner, and Seb had no doubt the cabinet beneath it held a variety of game consoles and games. He'd try to inspect those later. A cast-iron burner stood against the dividing wall between the living room and the place where Rutger was still asleep. The large dog bed, strategically placed close to the stove, made Seb smile. Nothing but the best for Raeynar, obviously.

He glanced at the dog, who still hadn't left his side. "Are you keeping me company or making sure I behave myself?" He scratched Raeynar between the ears.

As he walked along the hallway back to the bedroom, Seb noticed the prints hanging on the wall for the first time. They were stills from *Raeynar's Realm*, which had been Seb's favorite game long before he'd figured out that Rutger was its creator.

He arrived back where he'd started. One glance at the bed told him Rutger hadn't stirred. He'd just have a quick look at the one room he hadn't seen yet before rousing Rutger— possibly in more ways than one.

As soon as he opened the door to that last room, Seb

froze. He'd known Rutger was a famous game designer. But he hadn't realized that Rutger worked from home, so the collection of monitors, screens, computers, and other paraphernalia took him by surprise and left him awed. He took a few steps into the room, envy blossoming.

"Fuck." What it would be like to work in an office like this one. To have all that technology at his fingertips. Probably as amazing as being lucky enough to create games for a living. Putting together promotional videos, as Seb did, simply didn't compare.

"Is that a good fuck or a bad fuck?" Rutger's amused voice startled Seb.

"Definitely good. This is a fabulous setup." Seb turned and faced Rutger, who obviously and much to Seb's delight hadn't bothered putting on clothes when he got out of bed. "I'm sorry. I'm not snooping or anything. It's just you were still sleeping, and I got curious, and…"

"Hold it right there." Rutger raised his hand, laughter sparkling in his eyes. "If any part of my house was out of bounds, I would have told you so when we arrived."

Relief flooded Seb. Until Rutger found him, it hadn't even occurred to Seb that his curiosity might be rude.

"So, you approve?" Rutger's gaze moved around the room.

"I envy," Seb admitted.

"You're jealous? Why?" Rutger closed the distance between them, took Seb's hand, and pulled him along to the large desk featuring multiple monitors, a drawing pad, and various other high-tech toys that made Seb's finger itch.

A loud snort escaped Seb before he could stop it. "Because you appear to be living my dream." He sighed. "I've envied you ever since you mentioned you design games for a living. I'd happily sacrifice a limb to do your job." He gestured with his free hand. "And you get to work from home. You have all this space. You can get up and stretch your legs. Heck, you could share this office with a colleague, and you'd still have a wealth of space compared to the tiny cubicle I work in." The bitter note he discerned in his own voice didn't surprise Seb. He hadn't liked his job to begin with, and his boss's attitude was quickly eroding what little tolerance Seb had managed to hang on to up until now.

"Enough about work." Rutger turned and headed for the door, still holding Seb's hand. "Your break is short enough. How about a shower followed by lunch?" He glanced at Seb and raised his eyebrows.

"Sounds good." Seb grinned at Rutger. "How do you feel about water preservation?"

As they entered the bedroom, Rutger threw back his

head and laughed. "If that's your way of suggesting a joint shower, the answer is that I'm all for it." He opened the door opposite his bed.

"That's freaking awesome." Seb didn't think he'd ever seen a wet room like Rutger's outside of commercials and big-budget movies. It struck him that while Rutger's lifestyle might at first glance appear to be sober and basic, he clearly had high standards when it came to his work and comforts.

The bathroom was long and narrow. At the far end was a shower unlike anything Seb had ever been close to. For starters, it didn't have a head as such. Instead, there appeared to be a collection of perforated circles installed in the ceiling. The small silver fixings he noticed on two walls suggested water would be coming at them from the sides too.

"I'm glad you approve." Rutger smirked, but Seb thought he caught a note of relief in his voice. "Are you taking that off?" Rutger nodded at Seb's torso.

"What. Oh?" He'd completely forgotten he was wearing a shirt, just as it had somehow slipped his mind that he was otherwise naked. The moment the thought hit him, his cock filled and lengthened, which earned him an appreciative grunt from Rutger.

A few heartbeats later, Seb found himself under a deluge of water, leaning against Rutger, who had wrapped his arms around Seb's waist and pulled him close. He relaxed in Rutger's hold and turned his head to the water. It was bliss. Then it got better when Rutger stroked his belly with circular motions that got bigger on each rotation. The tips of Rutger's fingers brushed Seb's pubes, sending a delightful shiver through his body.

"You like that?" Rutger's voice was low, almost a growl.

Rather than reply, given that the answer was obvious, Seb pushed back with his arse, pressing it into Rutger's groin.

"You do." Rutger lowered his hand and stroked along Seb's almost fully erect cock with a couple of fingers.

"Yes." To emphasize his pleasure, Seb rocked against Rutger, eliciting a groan from him.

"You're so hot." Rutger wrapped his hand around Seb's dick and leisurely moved it up and down.

Seb sucked in a breath, as well as a mouth full of water. Rutger held both him and his cock in a tight grip during the resulting coughing fit.

"Maybe I should make you cough again," Rutger murmured as soon as Seb caught his breath. "The vibrations against my dick are something else."

Laughter escaped Seb, although he made sure to keep his face tilted down to avoid another near drowning.

"I've got an idea."

Before Seb could ask what Rutger had in mind, he felt his free hand between their bodies. Then Rutger's cock was lined up with Seb's butt crack.

"I like the way you think." Then Seb lost the power of speech as they fell into a rhythm, dictated by Rutger's hand on Seb's cock and eagerly matched by Seb's body. Seb reached back and pulled his arse cheeks apart. The slide of Rutger's dick through his crack felt naughty in a most delicious way.

"You feel so good. Do you feel my cock? How hard you make me?" Rutger switched from dirty talk to labored breathing and back again. "There's so much I want to do with you…to you." His grip on Seb's dick tightened. "Everything. I want it all."

"Yes!" Seb was so close his balls tingled. "Please. Everything." He wasn't sure what he was asking for; he just wanted more, for this to never stop. His body stiffened as his release hit him hard. He closed his eyes and sagged against Rutger as his second orgasm in as many hours raged through him.

"*Verdomme.*"

As Seb felt Rutger's cock jerk against his arse, he realized that was the first time Rutger had said something Seb didn't understand. In the back of his mind, he wondered where

Rutger had learned to speak English so well that Seb had forgotten it wasn't his first language. But postorgasmic bliss meant the question evaporated before he could peruse it, and he didn't chase it, content to lean into Rutger's hold and focus on nothing other than the man behind him, the torrent of water massaging them, and the pleasure they'd just given each other.

He could get used to this…if only he had more time.

Chapter Four

Rutger thanked his lucky stars—or maybe that should be his foresight— that he'd decided to serve a simple lunch. It had been some time since he'd felt as well and truly fucked as he did now. He laughed at himself under his breath. In the strictest sense of the word, they hadn't actually fucked yet.

He spooned the thick pea soup into two bowls and added them to the tray holding a basket containing a variety of breads and a butter dish. He hoped Seb would like it. It was all well and good serving a traditional Dutch winter dish. If Seb turned out to hate it, Rutger's best intentions would amount to nothing.

He carried the tray from the kitchen through the living room to the porch. From the corner of his eye, he noticed Seb on his knees with Raeynar by his side in front of the shelves containing his collection of computer games. He smiled. Considering how passionate Seb had been whenever they'd talked about games, it was hardly surprising he couldn't stay away from them.

As soon as he put the tray down, Rutger returned to the living room. Seb didn't give any indication that he'd noticed Rutger walking by him earlier or that he was aware of his presence now. Raeynar, on the other hand, hadn't missed Rutger passing them or the food he'd been carrying, and his tail thumped softly against the floor.

"Are you ready to eat?"

"Huh?" Seb got to his feet. "Sorry. I didn't see you there. But yes, I'm ready. Starving, actually. What are we having? Something smells good."

"It's a traditional soup we eat in winter. I hope you like it." It was silly to be nervous about a plain meal, but Rutger couldn't help himself. He wanted these two days to be perfect for Seb for mostly selfish reasons. Only a few hours after picking him up from the airport, Rutger was already regretting how brief Seb's visit would be. He was also mentally going over his schedule to work out when he might travel to stay with Seb. Shortly after they'd started chatting online, he'd suspected Seb was someone special, and nothing about their current encounter made him think he'd been wrong. Quite the opposite, in fact.

"That's a very impressive collection of games you've got there," Seb said as soon as they sat at the table, both facing the plot of land in front of Rutger's house where he'd parked his car. Raeynar, always the opportunist, had strategically taken up position between their chairs. "Although *Raeynar's Realm* is by far my favorite."

"Thank you." Rutger was shocked to discover how

much that statement pleased him. "Of course, you have to say that, seeing how you're staying with me." He winked while fervently hoping that Seb had meant what he said.

"I think I said as much before I discovered you created the game." Seb studied the thick green soup in his bowl as he spoke. "It's by far the best, most ingenious game I've ever played." He brought his spoon to his mouth and took a taste. "This is good." He immediately took another spoonful. "What did you say this is called?"

"I didn't." Rutger was glad the conversation had progressed from his game to their food. It was ridiculous how much Seb's words meant to him, and he wasn't ready to examine why Seb's opinion was so important. "It's called *erwtensoep* or *snert* for short, which translates as pea soup."

"Peas?" Seb frowned at his bowl before taking another spoonful. "I don't actually like peas."

Rutger laughed, grateful that his mouth was empty. As nice as the soup was, it wouldn't look good sprayed all over his windows. "Which is why I didn't tell you what it's called before you tried it."

"What's with the almost black bread?" Seb asked.

"It's rye bread and traditionally accompanies the snert. But as you can see, there are other options if you don't like it."

"Seeing I'm apparently engaged in a Dutch food

experiment, of course I'll try it." Seb took a slice, spread a liberal amount of butter on it, and took a bite. He chewed, swallowed, then stared at the slice in his hand for a moment before taking a second bite.

"Well? What do you think?"

"It's…different." Seb ate a little more. "A bit sour and very solid, but not bad at all."

"Phew." Rutger made a show of wiping his hand across his forehead.

"Why?" Seb chuckled. "Were you afraid I'd hate it?"

Rutger shrugged. "Not afraid, and I do have a variety of sandwich toppings in the fridge, in case you didn't like this."

"Well, I hope those toppings keep because this is amazing." As if he wanted to prove his point, Seb focused on his meal and didn't look at or speak to Rutger until his bowl was empty and he'd devoured another two slices of rye bread.

"That was good." Seb leaned back in his chair.

"Do you want more?" Rutger asked as he slipped a slice of smoked sausage to Raeynar.

"No, thank you. I'm stuffed." Seb patted his nonexistent belly.

"In that case, are you up for a walk?" Rutger stood and collected the plates, bowls, and butter dish.

"Sure." Seb got up too. "What did you have in mind?"

He picked up the tray before Rutger could and walked to the kitchen.

"Just to show you around," Rutger said as he followed Seb. "Introduce you to a little more of my world."

"So," Seb said twenty minutes later as they stood behind Rutger's house, ready to start their walk. "What is this place anyway?" He waved his hand, probably to indicate Rutger's house, the surrounding forest into which Raeynar had already disappeared, and the one other cabin they could just about see through the trees.

Rutger set off across the stretch of grass, heading for the narrow passage that led from his plot of land to the unsurfaced road a little farther along. "It used to be a private holiday place. When more and more people started taking foreign holidays, interest in renting cabins like mine for a full year at a time dwindled, and the owner decided to upgrade all the buildings and sell them to individuals who wanted to live in quiet, private surroundings."

The passage, created over decades by people who had taken a short cut to the backroad rather than any organized planning, led them around trees and bushes and forced them to watch where they were going if they wanted to avoid stumbling over tree roots.

"Apparently, the cottages and mobile homes didn't have either hot running water or electricity until a few years ago."

Seb snorted. "Seriously? How long have you been here?"

"Five years. The opportunity arose just when I started work on *Raeynar's Realm*."

"And before then, things were as primitive as you just described?"

Rutger chuckled. "I'm sure it wasn't too bad. I mean, if people only used the place as a holiday home, it might have even been a fun break from a person's normal way of life."

Seb turned his head and threw Rutger a sardonic glance, then instantly stumbled.

"Careful." Rutger managed to grab Seb's arm before he fell, the force of his reaction pulling Seb close.

Seb's eyes were a bit wide, and his lips were parted. The sight was too tempting for Rutger, so he kissed Seb. It was supposed to be a short connection of lips, but Seb's mouth was already familiar. Rutger was close to becoming addicted to his taste, so he took his fill because it wouldn't be long before he'd have to make do with video calls again. He wanted to gather memories for those occasions.

"Wow. Maybe I should trip again." Seb sounded a little breathless when they parted.

Laughter bubbled out of Rutger. "Don't go hurting yourself. If you want a kiss, just ask. There's plenty more where that came from." He took Seb's hand and set off again. It was all well and good joking about it, but if Rutger had anything to do with it, Seb wouldn't fall.

Once they reached the wider and smoother track, Rutger set a slow but steady pace. He pointed out other residences, mostly hidden from view, as they passed them, speeding up a little when they reached a house he didn't want to focus on.

"That used to be a public shower." Rutger indicated a wooden structure to their right. "From the more primitive days."

The road curved around a bend, and Seb came to an abrupt halt. "I didn't expect that."

"Good, isn't it?" Rutger stared at the round swimming pool in front of them.

"I don't suppose it's heated?" Seb asked, regret audible in his voice.

"Unfortunately not." It was one of the very few gripes Rutger had about this place. As soon as the water warmed a little in spring, he started swimming every morning, and he kept it up until the nights got frosty in autumn. "You like swimming?"

"Love it."

Surely the moment would come when they would run into something they completely disagreed about, but so far, Rutger had been shocked by how much they had in common. It had started with a common interest in games. But they'd soon discovered they also liked the same music, books, and movies.

"In that case, you'll have to come back in summer."

"Sure." Seb sounded deflated.

Damn. Rutger could have slapped himself. "I didn't mean I don't want you to come back before then. I just like the idea of swimming with you." He desperately wanted to lift the mood. "I bet you look good in Speedos."

Seb snorted. "I wouldn't know about that. Seeing how I don't own any." His eyes sparkled when he glanced at Rutger. "I guess I could get a pair."

"I think you should." Rutger winked and simultaneously swallowed his sigh of relief. He wanted Seb to feel welcome and eager to return. Maybe it didn't make sense after only a few hours, but having Seb in his house felt right.

They set off again and walked on until they reached the end of the backroad before turning right and, a short while later, right again to start their way home via the main road.

"Main road?" Seb laughed when Rutger used the term.

Rutger shrugged. Seb had a point, since this one wasn't

surfaced either. "It's the only way in and out of the estate by car. Hence main road."

The next few minutes, as they slowly made their way back to Rutger's house, they walked in silence. Raeynar darted in and out of the trees on both sides of the road, joining them for a few seconds before going off for another exploration or following a fascinating scent. At one point, they had to move to the side, pressing their backs against trees to allow a car to pass. The passengers waved at Rutger, who returned the gesture.

"Friends?" Seb asked when they resumed their journey.

"Depends on how you define the term," Rutger said. "There're only forty separate plots here, and most of us arrived at the same time. So I know and am friendly with everybody." He refrained from mentioning that his relationship with some didn't quite fit the word "friends."

"You've got it made here." Seb's voice held an edge of longing and envy. "You get to work from home, in a gorgeous location, and get on with all your neighbors, distant or not."

"But I don't have any pubs or other social outlets nearby," Rutger countered. He loved where he lived but was all too aware of the limitations associated with living in the middle of nowhere. "I'm not sure I would have settled here if I'd been ten years younger when the opportunity arose. I had to get socializing and clubbing out of my system first."

"I'm not sure a great social scene makes up for having to spend more than half my wages on rent every month. Not for a room in an apartment I have to share with people who weren't my choice as housemates."

They arrived back at Rutger's house, and Seb stopped walking. "If I could do my job from home, like you do, I would have moved away from Dublin ages ago."

Rutger didn't like how deflated Seb sounded. He'd hoped Seb would like his living arrangement, but the last thing he'd wanted to do was to bring Seb down. These two days were supposed to be joyful. He'd wanted to establish once and for all whether or not they were as drawn to each other in real life as they had been online. And while that certainly appeared to be the case, it amounted to nothing if Seb went back home unhappy.

"Let's get back inside. It may be my imagination, but I think the temperature is dropping." He took Seb's hand and pulled him along to the front door.

A sly grin erupted on Seb's face. "I can think of one or two ways to get warm again."

That's more like it. Rutger chuckled as they entered the cabin. "Can you now? Why don't you show me?"

Chapter Five

What the fuck is wrong with me? Seb cursed himself as they stepped into the comforting heat in Rutger's cabin. He had less than two days to spend with Rutger. Why was he spoiling them with complaints about his circumstances in Ireland? Sure, he was a little jealous of Rutger's life. But he could dwell on those feelings when he was home again. If he had any sense, he'd concentrate on enjoying himself, getting to know Rutger better, and making the most of the time they did have.

Those thoughts, as well as any dark feelings Seb harbored, vanished when Rutger took him into his arms and claimed Seb's mouth. The kiss was harsh, demanding, and quickly turned dirty when Rutger pumped his tongue in and out of Seb's mouth in a manner that left nothing to the imagination.

"I want you," Seb muttered when Rutger pulled back for a moment.

"How do you want me?" Ruther's eyes blazed with heat.

"Deep and hard," Seb said without hesitation. "Make me forget that I have another life for a while." Visiting Rutger was supposed to be a mini escape from everything Seb didn't like about his daily routine. Much to Seb's chagrin, it was turning into a reminder of everything his life lacked.

A grin as dirty as his kiss had been stretched across Rutger's face. "It will be my absolute pleasure." He headed for his bedroom, looking over his shoulder after two steps. "Are you coming, or am I doing this on my own?"

Laughter bubbled out of Seb, and his dismay evaporated. "And how exactly are you going to do that?"

Rutger winked at him. "I've got my ways." He grabbed Seb's hand and pulled him along. "But it's so much more fun with a real man."

Raeynar trotted along with them until Rutger ordered him to his bed. As much as Seb was getting attached to the dog, he was glad Raeynar wouldn't be joining them.

Before he'd even set foot in the bedroom, Seb had shed his coat and pulled his sweater and T-shirt over his head.

"Eager much?" Rutger sniggered, but his amusement didn't stop him from following Seb's example with obvious haste.

"What part of 'want you' do you not understand?" Seb kicked off his shoes and pushed his trousers and underpants down, making sure to also lose his socks. He glanced at Rutger, who'd just pulled his zipper down and was in the process of discarding his pants.

Seb was torn. Part of him wanted to watch and enjoy

the sight of Rutger stripping, drink it in, and seal it in his memory. A much bigger part couldn't wait to feel Rutger. He yearned for the stretch, the burn, and the sheer, bone-melting, and mind-blowing pleasure that would follow. He walked to the bed and stared at the small bedside tables on either side of it. "Where?"

"Second drawer of that cabinet in front of you." Rutger's voice was gruff and a little deeper than usual.

The lube and condoms were exactly where Rutger had said they would be. Seb grabbed them and dropped them on the bed before diving after them. He reached for the small container, but Rutger slapped his hand away.

"No, let me."

A thrill of excitement ran through Seb. Bossy Rutger was new, but Seb liked it. He liked it even better when Rutger pushed Seb's legs apart and knelt between them.

"*Zo mooi.*"

"What?" Going by Rutger's fixed gaze on Seb's groin area and the heat burning in his eyes, Seb had a suspicion of what those words might mean, but he wanted confirmation.

"So beautiful," Rutger said without looking up. He stroked a finger along the length of Seb's cock from the tip to the root before trailing it farther down and teasing Seb's balls. "And all mine." Still fully focused on Seb's dick, Rutger flipped the top of the lube container and held it upside down until the lotion trickled from Seb's balls into his arse crack. Then Rutger's finger was there too, rubbing the lotion in, stroking across Seb's perineum and hole, his touch light and maddingly enticing.

Desperate for more, Seb bucked his hips. The words "and all mine" had triggered a yearning deep inside him, something he didn't want to explore. Not now, not when his whole body craved Rutger. Only moments earlier, he had thought Rutger's need ran as deep as his, but now, frustratingly, it seemed that Rutger had all the time in the world and that he was determined to make use of it too.

"I know. I know." Rutger muttered the words as he continued his torturous exploration of Seb's erogenous zones. He pressed a finger against Seb's hole and breached him with just the tip.

"Yes!" Seb closed his eyes. "More."

As if Seb hadn't spoken—or maybe because he had, who knew?— Rutger retracted his fingertip before inserting it again. He kept this penetration shallow too. He repeated the action again and again until Seb felt torn between frustration and ecstasy.

"Please." Seb opened his eyes. "Rutger…Please."

A tender smile played on Rutger's lips as he stretched

and leaned forward to kiss Seb, who lifted his head and shoulders to meet him halfway. The combined movements pushed Rutger's finger deeper into Seb's arse. The only things stopping him from shouting out his delight were Rutger's mouth pressed against his and Rutger's tongue playing with Seb's.

If there was such a thing as heaven, surely this was it. Seb lost himself in a sea of pleasure and rode wave after sensual wave as Rutger's finger and tongue continued to drive him wild. Rutger added a second finger, and Seb lost it. He bucked on the bed, chasing Rutger's fingers for more, harder. His cock was like a steel rod on his tummy, and Seb fisted his hands to stop himself from touching it, convinced he would come instantly if he so much as stroked it.

Just when Seb thought he might climax anyway, Rutger withdrew his fingers, leaving Seb empty and bereft. The urge to beg for more was overwhelming. He pressed his lips together to keep the plea inside until the sound of a wrapper being torn reassured him. "Fuck, yeah. Need you." He fixed his gaze on Rutger's dick. It stood proud in its nest of dark blond hair with its head swollen and red. Rutger pushed the condom down, and Seb wished, with all his heart, there was no need for protection. Because suggesting going without would be stupid, Seb swallowed the thought. Who knew? If they got to do this again in the future, maybe they could get tested first.

Rutger took Seb's legs and pushed them up, then put his hand around the base of his cock. He stilled and looked from his cock to Seb's arse. *"Zo mooi."*

Seb was falling in love with those two words, but they vanished from his mind when Rutger breached him with his cock and slowly inched his way into Seb's yearning body. Despite the mind-blowing and seemingly endless foreplay, the stretch and the burn flared through Seb's body, and he welcomed them because they heralded the fulfillment of his wish.

"Take me. Hard and fast."

"So demanding." Rutger's chortle sounded breathless, and he obviously didn't mind following instructions because he pulled back the moment he bottomed out, only to plunge straight back in.

Their coming together was everything. Seb had fantasized about Rutger taking him; it had brought him to spectacular, self-generated orgasms on several occasions. Seb's imagination hadn't even come close to the breathtaking perfection of Rutger sliding in and out of him. Maybe it was because they'd been working towards this moment for months. Seb couldn't rule out that the brevity of his visit heightened his experience, but he had no doubt that being fucked had never felt this good before.

Rutger's mouth claimed Seb's again, his cock owned Seb's arse, and Rutger stroked his hand across Seb's belly in circles that increased in width with every rotation but failed to connect with his cock, while successfully spreading Seb's precum over his skin. He was everywhere. Rutger was the beginning and the end of Seb's world. Nothing else existed, just Rutger and his total possession of Seb's body and mind.

"So tight. Your hole was made for me." Rutger's breath came in bursts, his normally blue eyes were mostly black, and his voice was filled with awe.

"I'm close," Seb warned. He'd never come without his dick getting at least some attention, but he could feel the release building. His balls grew heavy and tingled, and his muscles tightened.

Rutger's large hand at last found Seb's cock and stroked it in time with his unrelenting invasion of Seb's arse.

Too much. Too good. Seb arched his back as his orgasm hit. While Rutger kept up a steady rhythm of invasion and withdrawal, burst after burst of cum hit Seb's chest and belly. It wasn't until Seb relaxed into the mattress again, suddenly loose-limbed, that Rutger erupted. Seb forced his eyes open and fixed his gaze on Rutger's face, still gorgeous despite being contorted from lust and need. Rutger threw back his head, his movements short and fast, and Seb felt his cock expand deep inside him.

Rutger came without a sound, but if his expression of wide-eyed wonder was anything to go by, this encounter had been as spectacular for Rutger as it had been for Seb.

"Fuck me," Rutger murmured as he dropped to the bed, thankfully making sure to land next to Seb.

"If you insist." Seb chuckled. "But you've got to give me a minute. I'm not *that* good."

"Funny man." Rutger turned his head and smiled at Seb with so much warmth and affection in his gaze goose bumps erupted on Seb's arms. Rutger reached to the side with his arm farthest away from Seb before wiping Seb's chest and tummy with something soft and wettish.

"What's with the baby wipes?" Seb asked. "Normal tissue not good enough for you?"

"Dry tissues aren't comfortable, and I'm too lazy to get out of bed and go to the bathroom after a good orgasm." Rutger tossed the wipe away without checking where it might land. "I wouldn't want to irritate all that beautiful skin."

Seb all but melted. *Don't get too attached. You're only here for one more day.* Seb detested the voice of reason shouting in his head but couldn't deny it had a point. This was supposed to be a fun interlude, not the beginning of something serious. How could it be with him living in Dublin and Rutger here in the Netherlands?

"What's wrong?" Rutger asked.

Shit. Obviously, Seb's face had betrayed at least some of his feelings. What did he say now? He couldn't tell Rutger he was falling for him much harder and faster than he could have anticipated. That if he'd known how perfect being with Rutger was, he might not have made the journey in the first place. How could Seb have predicted that attraction would turn into what looked suspiciously like feelings in such a short time?

"Nothing," Seb said eventually. "I just wish I could stay longer. These two days just aren't enough."

A sad yet tender smile appeared on Rutger's face, and he pulled Seb close until his head rested on Rutger's chest. "I know. But we'll make up for it. There's nothing stopping you from visiting again or me from getting on a plane to Ireland."

The flash of delight Seb experienced burned out almost instantly when he remembered that he was in no position to offer Rutger a place to stay. They'd never discussed their living arrangements during their chats, and now that he'd seen Rutger's house, Seb was even less inclined to share the paltry measurements of the one room he called his own. Grateful that Rutger couldn't see his face at the moment, Seb said nothing. If and when Rutger announced he was coming to Dublin, it would be early enough to explain to him that they needed to make alternate sleeping arrangements.

Rutger's heart thumped quietly beneath Seb's ear, and Rutger's soft, rhythmic strokes across his back soothed Seb. He relaxed. He wasn't going to spoil what little time they had together by worrying about what might happen. He snuggled closer and smiled against Rutger's chest when he tightened his grip and gathered him in. It would be so easy to get used to this, to imagine a life with Rutger and Raeynar, right here in this cabin.

As if he was a mind reader, Raeynar jumped onto the bed and settled in the spot between Rutger's and Seb's feet. For a moment Seb wondered how the dog had known when it was safe for him to join the humans, then decided that it didn't matter. It was good, close to perfect even. And yes, getting used to this was all too easy and a very bad idea.

Chapter Six

When Rutger opened his eyes, he had no idea what time it was or how long he'd been asleep. The room was shrouded in darkness, but that didn't tell him a lot, since at this time of year the sun set at about half past four in the afternoon. He reached over and flicked on the lamp on his bedside table.

Zo mooi.

Seb lay curled up beside him with the covers pulled up to his chin and his arse pressing into Rutger's thigh. His unruly black hair made a stark contrast against the white pillowcase.

Reluctant to wake Seb up just yet, despite the brevity of their time together, Rutger drank him in. He'd felt a connection with Seb from the moment they'd started sending each other direct messages, and the link had only grown stronger as they progressed to phone and video calls. He could vividly remember the first time they'd shared hand jobs while online and how Rutger had longed to get his hands on Seb.

I'm going to miss you.

The realization came as somewhat of a surprise. Prior to Seb's arrival, Rutger had been afraid that a real-life encounter might shatter the illusion, that Seb wouldn't live up to the image Rutger had created in his mind. He'd worried about nothing. If anything, he was more attracted to Seb now than he'd been before. He hated that in about twenty-four hours they would say goodbye again. Even if they arranged for a follow-up trip, there would be a gap of weeks—if not months—before Rutger would get to hold Seb again.

He reached out and stroked Seb's hair away from his forehead. Rutger had no intention of saying as much out loud, but he wanted to keep Seb. It didn't seem likely, but if Seb was only in it for a few hours of fun between the sheets—and there was no denying Rutger had been having great fun—Rutger would be devastated. He sighed before propping himself up on one arm, leaning forward and pressing his lips against Seb's cheek. A light prickle of stubble that hadn't been there earlier teased Rutger.

"Hmmmmm." The sound of appreciation Seb uttered without opening his eyes made Rutger smile. He had to stop focusing on the end of their get-together and start enjoying every single minute they had.

Seb rolled onto his back and blinked his eyes open. "Hey." The sleepy smile playing on his face made him look adorable.

"Hey, you too." Rutger kissed Seb on the lips. "There's no need for you to get up. I'm going to throw some dinner together for us. I just didn't want you to wake up on your own."

"Can I help?" Despite his offer, Seb sounded only half-awake.

"No. It's as good as done. I just have to reheat it. Stay here, and I'll come and get you when everything's ready."

"Time is it?" Seb asked.

Rutger chuckled. Despite it being his first thought when he woke up, he still hadn't checked how long they had slept. "I'm not sure. After five, but that's all I can tell you." He pulled back the covers and got out of bed, searching through the various items of clothing on the floor for his pants. When he found them, he extracted his phone.

"Damn."

"What?" Seb sat up in the bed, suddenly wide awake and with a concerned expression on his face.

"I didn't think we'd slept that long." Rutger wanted to kick himself. There was no point worrying about how little time they had when they were going to sleep away hours they could have spent in much better ways. "It's almost eight o'clock."

"Bollix." Seb jumped out of bed and reached for his underpants. "We slept away hours. And we have so few of them."

Despite being annoyed with himself for losing track of time, Rutger smiled. Seb had more or less voiced Rutger's thoughts word for word. And not for the first time. While it didn't give them extra time together, it was gratifying to see Seb treasure every minute they did have as much as Rutger did.

Raeynar bounded ahead of them as they made their way to the kitchen.

"There's really nothing to do for you here," Rutger said. "If you want to go inside and get comfortable…"

Seb snorted. "I've been comfortable for far too long already. Unless I'm in the way, I prefer to stay here." He leaned against the floor-to ceiling-cupboard and crossed his arms.

As he placed the bowl in the microwave oven, Rutger smiled to himself. It delighted him to see Seb so reluctant to be separated, even if it only was by a few meters and one room.

"What are we having anyway?" Seb asked. "Another Dutch dish?"

Rutger opened the oven, took out the mixture, and stirred it before putting it back. "It's called *boerenkool*. I've no idea what that might be in English."

"Let me see." Seb looked over Rutger's shoulder. "That looks like colcannon." He looked at Rutger as if he expected him to confirm the identification. "A mixture of kale and potatoes?"

"So, there is an English name for it. I'll have to remember that."

"Actually," Seb said. "I think colcannon is an Irish

thing."

The oven dinged, and Rutger took the bowl out. "Since you're here anyway, would you mind grabbing two plates and some cutlery?" He nodded in the direction of the cupboard Seb had been leaning against. He waited until Seb had gathered what they needed before leading the way to the dinner table on the patio.

"And what's this?" Seb prodded the meat with his fork.

"Smoked sausage. It was in your soup earlier too." Rutger chuckled. "We eat a lot of it in winter."

After he cut off a slice and speared it with his fork, Seb inspected the sausage before putting it in his mouth. "Oh. That's not bad." He took another bite. "Not bad at all, in fact." He took a forkful of the potato and kale mixture. "All of this is good."

They spent the next few minutes eating in silence, with only the scrape of knives and forks on plates disturbing the peace.

"Tell me," Seb said after he'd cleared his plate and as he passed his last slice of sausage to Raeynar. "What do Dutch people do to celebrate the New Year?"

Damn. Rutger couldn't believe he hadn't mentioned that yet. "I've been meaning to talk to you about that. Sit down inside while I put this away." He stood. "Would you like something to drink? Coffee?"

"Coffee sounds good." Seb got up too. "And now I'm curious. Do you want a hand?"

"Nope. You've done your share of the work when you got on that plane and came here. Now it's my turn." Rutger smiled at Seb.

The warmth in Seb's gaze took Rutger's breath away. He quickly gathered the dirty dinnerware and walked to the kitchen before he said something Seb might not want to hear.

What was wrong with him? This was meant to be a fun, uncomplicated visit. An opportunity to get to know each other better and enjoy in person what they'd so far only been able to see. He wasn't supposed to be falling for Seb. Except that ship appeared to have sailed. Rutger was falling hard and fast. He'd no intention of telling Seb because he couldn't imagine Seb's feelings matching his, but Rutger was sure Seb would be taking a large part of Rutger's heart with him when he returned to Dublin.

He switched on his coffee maker and filled the dishwasher while the water heated. There wasn't a whole lot he could do about his feelings, of course. They were what they were. But he could and should make sure that Seb had no idea of what was going on in Rutger's head and heart. Not now, anyway. Maybe, at some point in the future, if Rutger's feelings stayed the same once they were separated again, he could make a confession. Opening his mouth now came with the very real risk of ruining the limited hours still left to them, and he had no intention of doing that.

By the time he entered the living room carrying a tray, Rutger had regained his calm. He placed the tray on the wooden chest functioning as a side table and picked up a mug filled with black coffee for himself, then sat on the couch. "Wanna join me?" He patted the cushion beside him.

"Sure." Seb, who had knelt in front of the collection of computer games again, got up, crossed the floor, and sank down next to Rutger.

"Help yourself." Rutger nodded at the coffee. "You asked me how we celebrate New Year's Eve here."

"So I did." Seb leaned forward, took the remaining cup, and sat back again.

"Apart from the usual, you know, staying up until midnight, kissing and hugging people you barely know while wishing them the best for the coming year, the one big thing in the Netherlands is fireworks."

"Like big displays?" Seb asked, sounding excited. "With music and all?"

"Not really." Rutger thought for a moment. "We have those too. But on New Year's Eve, from ten until two, fireworks can be legally set off by anybody."

"Anybody?" Seb stared at Rutger. "Wow."

"Do you not have fireworks in Ireland?" Rutger asked.

Laughter bubbled out of Seb. "Sure, we do. And there's no shortage of loud bangs and flares and what-have-you on New Year's Eve and Halloween. But none of it is legal." He took a sip from his coffee. "This is good." He drank some more. "So, will there be fireworks here tonight? Do you have any?" Seb's eyes were wide and shone with excitement.

As much as Rutger hated fireworks, he was sorry to disappoint Seb. "No. We—and by that I mean the people living on the estate—agreed early on to forgo fireworks. For starters, most of us own dogs, and they hate loud noises. It's also a bit dodgy, what with all the trees and such." He drank from his mug. "But we do organize a bonfire every year. It starts around ten o'clock and lasts through midnight."

"Are we going?" Seb asked, less excited than he'd been before but still looking interested.

"If you feel like it." Rutger wasn't sure what he wanted Seb's answer to be. He knew it would be a good party, and he was just as sure that he and Seb would be welcomed with open arms. In fact, at least one person would give him a hard time if he failed to make an appearance. But with so little time left before Seb had to leave again…Rutger just didn't know.

Seb said nothing as he sipped from his coffee. He

glanced at Rutger, then focused on his drink again. Rutger would have given just about anything to be able to read his mind right now, to find out if Seb's dilemma was the same as his. As it was, all he could do was wait.

"We wouldn't have to stay too long, would we?" Seb asked eventually.

Rutger bit back the grin that threatened to erupt on his face. It was ridiculous how happy he was because Seb obviously shared his reluctance to eat into their limited time together.

"I mean, I wouldn't mind meeting some of your friends. And I've never been to a proper bonfire." Seb continued as if he thought Rutger needed to be convinced.

"Never been to a bonfire?" Rutger was aghast.

Seb shrugged. "They weren't allowed or encouraged in the housing estate where I grew up. Sure, I've seen neighborhood kids burn stuff in the middle of a field, but those fires were small and never lasted long because well, they were illegal."

"That settles it. We're going to the party tonight. You're right. We don't have to stay for long. He placed his mug on the table, and when he saw Seb had finished his coffee, Rutger took his cup too. When he straightened, he wrapped his arm around Seb's shoulders and pulled him along as he settled into the cushions.

Perfection. What could be better than relaxing in his house while a fire roared in the stove, Raeynar basked in the heat on his bed near the burner, and an attractive, sexy, and fascinating man kept him company?

"Tell me about Dublin?" Rutger wanted to know more about Seb, everything, and that included where he came from. It only occurred to him now how little they knew about each other. How had they managed to interact online for months without getting into personal details? He knew all about the books Seb liked to read, his taste in music, and the games he preferred, but very little else.

"You've never been to Ireland?"

"Once. Two years ago." Rutger snorted. "For a visit even shorter than yours now. I arrived on the first flight of the day and flew back home on the last. I was there for business, and I didn't see a thing except the road between the airport and the conference center." He reconsidered. "And rain. I don't think it stopped at all while I was there."

Seb laughed. "That's why they call us the Emerald Isle. All that water keeps us green."

"There's nothing green about you." Rutger lifted his hand from Seb's shoulder and pressed softly against his cheek until he turned his head enough for Rutger to kiss him.

The kiss was lazy and tender. As amazing as it was, they

appeared to be on the same page again. Neither pushed for more or turned up the heat. Rutger relished the press of Seb's lips against his, the intimate play of their tongues; he imagined he could live on the taste of Seb. He closed his eyes and focused on the magic they created and tried to commit the sheer wonder of it to his memory. When at last they pulled apart, Rutger rested his forehead against Seb's. *I'm going to miss you.*

Chapter Seven

It was, of course, ridiculous to be nervous about going to an informal party. A bonfire, for crying out loud. It didn't get much more casual than that. Unfortunately, the butterflies in Seb's stomach hadn't received that memo. His heart beat a little too fast as Seb and Rutger walked along the road, Raeynar trotting along beside them. Rutger had put a leash on the dog while explaining that they might still hear fireworks being set off elsewhere and that he didn't want Raeynar to run off in fear.

Back home, Seb never hesitated before walking into a pub or club on his own. He didn't have a problem approaching strangers or starting a conversation. Yet here he was, on tenterhooks because he was going to meet Rutger's friends.

"Are you okay?" Rutger sounded concerned.

"Sure. Why?"

"If you squeeze my fingers any tighter, you'll cut off the circulation." A note of bemusement crept into Rutger's voice.

Bollix. Seb wanted Rutger's friends to like him. There was no need for Rutger to know that, though, or that Seb didn't want to disappoint him.

"Sorry." Loosening his grip was an effort, but Seb

managed it.

"I should probably tell you that you'll meet my mother tonight."

Wait. What? If Seb had been nervous before, it had been nothing compared to the explosi0n of butterflies in his belly now. "Your parents will be at the bonfire?" Seb was proud that his voice didn't betray his apprehension.

"Just my mother."

"She lives here too?"

"In the big house overlooking the fields we walked by earlier."

"Why didn't you say anything?" It seemed a strange thing to have kept quiet about when Rutger had pointed out other features like old shower houses and the pool.

"Because I wanted to sneak by her house without being seen," Rutger said. "If she'd spotted us, she would have invited us in, and we would have wasted at least an hour making polite conversation."

The note of embarrassment in Rutger's voice forced Seb to bite back his smile. This version of Rutger came across as a lot younger than thirty-nine, and it was endearing.

"She knows I'm here, then," Seb asked. Seb wasn't sure what to think or feel. Rutger obviously wasn't concerned about introducing Seb to his mother, so Seb should be able to be calm about it too. On the other hand, meeting parents was something Seb associated with long-term relationships. In fact, he'd never brought a boyfriend to meet his family.

Rutger nodded.

"Wow."

"What?" Rutger sounded confused.

"If my mother knew I was anywhere near her with a… another man, she would find an excuse to join us and satisfy her curiosity." He'd almost said partner instead of "another man." It was too early to think of Rutger in those terms, and it didn't make sense. Even if Rutger felt the same, they would still be hundreds of miles apart. Long-distance relationships had a bad reputation for a reason. They were hard to maintain.

"I asked her not to," Rutger said simply, as if it explained everything.

Seb opened his mouth to say that such a request wouldn't have stopped *his* mother when the smell of wood burning hit his nose, and he saw a glimmer of orange in front of them, to the right. A few steps later, he could see more of the fire, and voices filtered through the night air as well as the sound of somebody strumming a guitar. Excitement of the good variety bubbled up in Seb. Whatever happened next, this would be a memorable New Year's Eve.

An hour later, Seb admitted to himself that he'd worried about nothing. He and Rutger had been welcomed enthusiastically, and while people had shown an interest in Seb and what he thought about their community, they hadn't been obviously curious about him or his relationship with Rutger. As for Rutger's mother, she was an absolute delight. It had started when she'd introduced herself as Merel, saving Seb from having to try and pronounce Kneynsberg, the family name she shared with Rutger. Seb's nerves had mostly calmed down, but he was determined not to make himself look foolish.

"It's a shame you couldn't come for longer, Sebastian," Merel said. They sat on a wooden bench, Raeynar asleep at their feet, close enough to the fire to benefit from the heat but not so near they had to worry about sparks reaching them. "I would have loved to have had you and Rutger over for dinner and to get to know you a little better."

"Mam." Rutger managed to put a strong note of warning in that one word.

"What?" Merel laughed. "This is the first time you've invited someone to stay with you. Of course, I'm curious."

First time? Seb wondered what, if anything, that meant. Rutger had said he'd moved into his cabin five years ago. If Seb really was his first overnight visitor, that had to mean something, didn't it? Seb focused on the fire, studiously avoiding both Merel's and Rutger's gaze. He didn't want them to notice how much that statement delighted him. Besides, Merel was probably exaggerating. Rutger had been so eager to welcome Seb it was hard to imagine Rutger having lived in isolation until now.

Merel turned to Seb. "Let's ignore my son for a moment." She smiled. "I want to know more about you. All Rutger would tell me is that you're Irish."

"Mam!" Irritation crept into Rutger's voice as he continued to talk to his mother. Since he was speaking Dutch, Seb had no idea what he might be saying, although he had his suspicions. It was obvious, however, that whatever he was saying wasn't making much of an impression on Merel.

"It's okay." Seb reached out and placed his hand on Rutger's arm, squeezing softly. "I don't mind talking about any of that." He focused on Merel, who smiled affectionately. When he followed her gaze, Seb noticed it was fixed on his hand on Rutger's arm.

"I live and work in Dublin," Seb began, "as do my parents."

"And are you working in the same field as Rutger?" Merel asked.

"I wish."

The wide-eyed stare his reply earned him from both Merel and Rutger indicated that Seb might have reacted a bit too strongly.

"No, I don't work in the same field," Seb continued in a more subdued tone of voice. "I work as a graphic designer for a marketing company. It's not a bad job."

"But it's not what you would be doing if you could have it your way." Merel added the words Seb had swallowed.

"Something like that," Seb agreed. He took a sip of beer from the green bottle he'd been handed shortly after arriving. He suddenly regretted that he'd agreed to answer Merel's questions. He didn't want to focus on everything that wasn't perfect about his life back in Ireland and spoil his limited time here as a result.

"Merel!" The woman who'd been softly strumming on the guitar since they arrived called out.

"I guess the rest of my questions will have to wait," Merel grinned at Seb. "Duty calls." She got up and joined the guitarist.

"I'm sorry about that," Rutger said softly.

"Don't worry about it." Seb squeezed Rutger's thigh. "That's nothing compared to the interrogation my mother would give you if I brought you for a visit. Trust me. She makes the Spanish Inquisition look like amateurs."

"And no one expects the Spanish Inquisition." Rutger chuckled.

"Exactly." Seb laughed along, delighted that Rutger had picked up on the Monty Python reference. "Maybe it comes with the job description," he added.

"Job description?"

"I don't know," Seb said. "Maybe interrogating their kids' friends is what mammies are supposed to do."

"I'm thirty-nine years old." Rutger sounded indignant. "I don't need my mother vetting my lover, thank you very much."

Too caught up in being overjoyed that Rutger referred to him as his lover, Seb had no idea how to respond. Thankfully Seb didn't have to worry about it, since the guitarist picked that moment to start playing louder. A clear and melodious voice almost immediately added words to the tune.

Merel sang in what Seb assumed was Dutch, so he had no idea what the song was about, but he had no problem recognizing how beautiful her voice was. "Wow. Your mother is good."

"I should hope so." Rutger stared at his mother with love and pride in his eyes. "A professional singer who can't hold a tune would be a disaster."

"Professional?" Seb was impressed.

"For as long as I can remember." Rutger didn't take his eyes off his mother as he spoke. "She sang in a band when I was younger. These days she performs in theatrical productions. Musicals and such."

They fell silent and listened to the music as Merel and the guitarist tackled a variety of songs, all of them as gorgeous as they were new and incomprehensible to Seb. When Rutger put his arm around Seb's shoulder and pulled him close, Seb closed his eyes and lost himself in the tunes while the flames from the fire created colors behind his eyelids.

Seb was close to drifting off when he recognized the starting chords of the next song. He straightened abruptly, dislodging Rutger's arm.

"What's wrong?" Rutger sounded concerned.

"Nothing. I know this song. It's *The Red Rose Café.*"

"Not in Dutch, it isn't." Rutger chuckled. "How come you know a Dutch song?"

"I don't. I know this song in English." When the chorus started, Seb sang along softly about the café in Amsterdam's harbor.

"You've got a good voice too," Rutger remarked when Seb fell silent. When the chorus started again, Rutger added, "sing it louder."

Self-conscious but reluctant to refuse, Seb raised his

voice as he sang along. Much to his horror, Merel fell silent and allowed him to finish the chorus on his own. A short but spontaneous round of applause when he stopped singing relieved some of Seb's embarrassment.

"I didn't know there is a Dutch version of that song," Seb remarked when the guitarist and Merel announced they were stopping because it was almost midnight.

Rutger laughed. "I think you will find the Dutch *version* predates yours by at least a decade."

Before Seb could react, a loud cheer went up, and people were embracing each other with shouts of something Seb assumed meant "Happy New Year."

"*Gelukkig Nieuwjaar*," Rutger said, confirming Seb's suspicion about what he'd heard. He placed his hand against Seb's cheek and turned his head for a deep kiss.

"Happy New Year," Seb replied when they withdrew. "At least, I think that's what you said."

"Right the first time." Rutger got up. "I guess I'd better do the rounds." He handed Seb the leash. "You keep an eye on Raey for me. I'll be right back."

Both Raeynar and Seb followed Rutger with their eyes as he walked from person to person, hugging some, exchanging kisses with others. Seb wondered why Dutch people apparently kissed each other on the cheeks three times. Why not twice? Or four times? He leaned forward and petted Raeynar, stupidly delighted that the dog had been happy to keep him company and didn't appear to be pining for Rutger.

"Happy New Year." Merel appeared at Seb's side, seemingly out of nowhere.

He got to his feet and, much to his surprise, found himself exchanging three cheek kisses with Rutger's mother.

"You're a good singer," Merel said once they were seated again.

"I don't know about that," Seb replied with a smile. "I know how to hold a tune, but that's about it."

Merel laughed. "Holding a tune counts for a lot. But I think you sounded better than that."

"Thank you." Seb felt humbled. The compliment meant a lot coming from someone who was a professional.

"I hope you're not interrogating him again." Rutger frowned at his mother when he returned.

"She isn't." Seb loved how protective Rutger appeared to be of him, but he didn't want to cause trouble between mother and son.

Merel's bright laughter rang out again. "Showing interest hardly constitutes an interrogation. Does it?" She raised her eyebrows at Seb.

He shook his head. "It didn't bother me."

"Good." Merel stood. "I just came by to say good night. I'm going home." She turned to Seb. "It was nice meeting you. I hope it won't be too long before I see you again." Her smile was warm and appeared genuine.

"So do I." Seb watched Merel as she circled the fire before disappearing between the trees. *So do I.*

"Maybe we should follow her example," Rutger suggested a moment later. "The fire is dying down, so unless we move, we'll be freezing soon."

Seb stared at the bonfire, and as soon as he saw that Rutger was right, a shiver ran down his spine. As if his body had needed the visual reminder that it was both after midnight and midwinter. He yawned. Obviously, he was more tired than he'd realized too.

Rutger held out his hand. When Seb grabbed it, Rutger pulled him along away from what remained of the party.

"Shouldn't we say goodbye to everybody?" Seb asked, fervently hoping the answer would be no. He'd enjoyed the evening more than he'd thought he might, but he was ready to be alone with Rutger again. They were fast running out of time.

Rutger walked on without relinquishing Seb's hand. "There's no need for such formalities."

A wave of contentment flowed through Seb as they slowly made their way back to Rutger's cottage. Between the cold night air, Rutger's hand in his, and Raeynar trotting along beside him, Seb was simply happy. When tiny specks of white flowed from the sky, Seb tilted his head back and laughed. Snowflakes tickled his cheeks and lips and made the already awesome day and night perfect.

"I love snow." Seb grinned at Rutger. "And most years we don't get any in Ireland."

Rutger chuckled. "Don't get too excited. The Netherlands isn't known for cold winters either. Even if it does stick, chances are we'll get little more than a dusting, and it will be gone again before noon tomorrow."

"Spoilsport." Seb's fatigue had vanished to be replaced by a giddiness that made him feel like a child. "As long as we get enough for a snowball fight when we get up."

"I'll set my alarm."

Seb wasn't sure if Rutger was teasing him, but it didn't matter. Nothing Rutger might say could break the magic of the moment. The arrival of snow was like the icing on an already fabulous cake. This time with Rutger had been amazing before now, and this added yet another wonderful memory to what was turning into an unforgettable trip.

If only it didn't have to end.

Chapter Eight

"Holy fuck!"

The exclamation pulled Rutger from a deep sleep.

"It will only be a dusting, he said. We don't get cold winters either. Right."

"Who're you talking to?" Rutger mumbled without opening his eyes.

"Myself, I thought. Obviously, I was wrong." Seb sounded amused and disturbingly awake. "You need to see this. It's amazing."

Resigned to the fact that he wouldn't be getting any more sleep, Rutger opened his eyes and immediately closed them again. The light in his bedroom was harsh and bright. He tried again, making sure to squint through his lashes this time, and saw Seb standing in front of the window, stark naked. The sight was more than glorious enough to clear Rutger's mind and banish the last tendrils of sleep. He threw back the covers and stepped out of bed, shivering as his feet touched the floor.

"What has you so excited?" he asked as he crossed the floor to join Seb. The moment he glanced out of the window, he received his answer. "Holy fuck indeed." The clearing behind his house was covered in a thick blanket of snow. It was hard to judge exactly how much had fallen, but what he saw outside was a lot more than the light sprinkling he'd predicted.

"Isn't it great?" Seb's eyes sparkled, and the enthusiasm on his face made him look younger than his twenty-six years. "Let's go outside." He turned and walked to the door.

"You may want to put some clothes on first." Rutger chuckled.

"What?" Seb halted and looked down. "Oh." He grinned at Rutger. "I'd forgotten I was naked."

For reasons he wasn't going to explore right now, it made Rutger ridiculously happy that Seb was comfortable enough around him to be unaware of his state of undress.

Seb strode to the corner of the room where he'd dropped his holdall the day before, knelt, and extracted what looked like a pair of jogging pants and a sweatshirt from it. He glanced at Rutger over his shoulder. "Don't just stand there. Get dressed! There's snow to be played with."

With a bemused shake of his head, Rutger went to his wardrobe. He selected clothes similar to those Seb had pulled from his bag and put them on, not bothering with underwear. Everything he wore would almost certainly end up soaking wet, so less was probably better.

A few minutes later, after they'd added coats, scarves, and gloves to the clothes they'd thrown on, Rutger tried to open his front door, only to discover he had to put his weight behind the motion. The snow outside was high and heavy enough to have created an obstruction. As soon as he managed to push the door free, Raeynar flashed by him and instantly disappeared into the snow up to his belly. Rutger laughed as the dog pushed his snout into the snow before shaking it off and barking as if he was affronted by it. Rutger felt pressure against his back and launched forward, landing on his knees in the snow.

"Hey." He grabbed a hand full of snow before turning towards a grinning Seb. "I'll get you for that." He squeezed the powder into a ball and threw it at Seb, laughing out loud when it hit him midchest.

Next thing Rutger knew, Seb landed on top of him, and they were rolling in the white fluffy blanket and trying to shove hands full of freezing flakes down the back of each other's coats. It was childish and stupid and the most fun Rutger had had in ages. It got even better when they introduced kissing to their play fight. The combination of Seb's hot mouth pressed against his and the freezing snow melting against his back drove Rutger crazy. Only when Raeynar joined in the madness, alternately licking his or Seb's face before rushing off again, barking excitedly, did they pull their mouths apart.

Seb dropped down beside Rutger with a contented sigh. "That was good."

Rutger couldn't argue with that statement. He hadn't been aware of missing out, but maybe his routine had become a bit stale and regimented over the past few years. It was good to have Seb here. He'd needed the reminder that there was more to life than work, that it was okay to have fun just for the sake of enjoying himself. *I'm going to miss him.* He turned his head and found Seb staring at him with what looked like a wistful expression on his face. *"Will you miss me too?"* As much as he wanted to know the answer, Rutger refused to voice the question. He would be devasted if Seb didn't feel the same, and if Seb's feelings *did* match his, it wouldn't change the fact that a few hours from now their time together would be over.

Shit. Rutger sat up and looked at his car. Going to the airport might turn into an issue. The snowdrift reached the car's bumper. The road was covered in virgin snow, without a single tire track. There was absolutely no way Rutger would be able to drive under these circumstances.

Excitement fluttered in Rutger's stomach. If he couldn't drive, Seb wouldn't be able to leave. Rutger wasn't prepared for how much he wanted Seb to stay and didn't like how selfish his thoughts were. Seb had a job and a life to return to. Unfortunately, Rutger's desire to hang on to Seb didn't change that reality.

"How about we go in and have breakfast?" He asked,

more to stop his thoughts from further upsetting him than because he was hungry. Besides, he fully expected a thaw to set in any moment now. He'd been amazed to see all the pristine snow when he woke up, but experience told him it wouldn't last.

"Sure." Seb got up. "I think I could do with dry clothes." He laughed. "This is great. I've only seen this much snow once before."

Rutger stood too and followed Seb into the house, whistling for Raeynar as he went.

"Will you look at that?" Seb stood on the porch, staring through the window. "More snow."

Rutger stepped up behind Seb and wrapped his arms around his waist. Sure enough, white flakes were dropping steadily from the sky. "Beautiful, isn't it?"

"Yes." Seb turned his head, kissed the side of Rutger's mouth, and focused on the view again.

The moment was so simple and yet so magical. Rutger pulled Seb closer and rested his chin on Seb's shoulder, and for long, peaceful moments, they just stood there, staring at the world outside as it got whiter. Then Seb shivered.

"Let's get out of these wet clothes." Rutger turned around without releasing Seb and pushed him in the direction of the bedroom. Raeynar, by far the most sensible of them, lay on his bed in front of the fire, soaking up the heat.

They undressed quickly and without ceremony. Now wasn't the time for a sexy striptease or slowly peeling garments off each other. When they were both naked, Rutger took their clothes. "Wait here." He smiled at Seb before returning to the living room, extracting the fold-up clothes airer from a cupboard on the way. He placed it next to the stove, making sure not to disturb Raeynar, and draped their wet attire over the rack. Walking away from a naked Seb wasn't easy, but common sense had prevailed. If at all possible, Seb's garb should be dry before he packed it.

Fully expecting Seb to be dressed again, Rutger was happily surprised when he found a stark-naked Seb sitting on the edge of his bed. His cheeks were still rosy from the cold, but his cock obviously hadn't suffered from the freezing temperatures, judging by its proud stance. Indeed, Seb leisurely moving his hand up and down his shaft might have something to do with his erection. The sight was more than enticing enough to rush blood to Rutger's dick.

"Come here to me." Seb's voice was low and a little rough as he spread his legs and indicated the space between them

It was the easiest order in the world to follow, and Rutger didn't waste any time.

"I can't believe I haven't tasted you yet," Seb

murmured before leaning forward and swiping his tongue across the head of Rutger's, now mostly hard, cock.

Rutger watched Seb as he unhurriedly investigated the length of Rutger's dick with his tongue and mouth, wondering how he'd gotten so lucky. Seb looked up at him, his huge blue eyes filled with heat, before parting his lips and sliding his mouth down Rutger's cock.

"Jesus." It had been a while since Rutger's last blow job, but he didn't remember it as being anywhere near as good as this experience. Either Seb was gifted, or there was something else, something more, in play. Rutger couldn't focus on the dilemma as Seb's rhythmic bobbing movements pushed his cock ever deeper into Seb's mouth until Seb's nose connected with Rutger's pubes.

Seb pulled off. "Good?" His mouth was back on Rutger's cock almost before he finished his one-word question.

"Perfect." Unable to resist the urge, Rutger moved his hips. Seb didn't appear to mind having his face fucked and stilled, allowing Rutger to set the pace while sucking hard and teasing Rutger's sensitive shaft with his tongue.

It was so fucking good. But it wasn't enough. With great reluctance, Rutger stepped back.

"What's wrong?" Seb's wide eyes betrayed his confusion.

"Absolutely nothing." Rutger stroked a finger across Seb's swollen lips. "But I'm feeling left out. Lie down." He pointed at the bed.

Clearly still unsure what was happening, Seb did as instructed. When Rutger joined him on the bed in such a position that both their mouths were opposite the other's cock, Seb chuckled. "I like this idea." Then Seb's mouth was back where it, as far as Rutger was concerned, belonged.

Rutger didn't waste a moment and sucked the tip of Seb's dick into his mouth and used his tongue to circle it and tease the tiny hole.

A muffled and indistinct sound escaped Seb, and, encouraged, Rutger sucked harder.

Heaven. Rutger reached for Seb's balls and fondled them as he took Seb deeper. Seb copied Rutger's actions, and they fell into an enticing and heat-building rhythm. Rutger wasn't sure who was setting the pace or even if either of them was. All he knew was the mind-blowing pleasure of feeling Seb's warm mouth massaging his cock and the enticing taste of Seb on his tongue. They were in sync as if this wasn't the first time they indulged in this delightful exercise.

Heat like molten lava flowed through in Rutger's veins. His world reduced to Seb's cock in his mouth, Seb's mouth on Rutger's dick, and Seb's hand massaging Rutger's balls and stroking a finger over his perineum. Rutger was moments away from coming, and he doubled his efforts. As unlikely as he knew it was, he desperately wanted them to come together.

Rutger stilled with his cock deep in Seb's mouth when his orgasm hit. A heartbeat later, the bitter taste of Seb's release hit Rutger's tongue. So good. So perfect. *Why can't I keep him?*

Seb pressed his lips against Rutger's thigh, then chuckled.

"What?" Rutger asked, already smiling, although he had no idea what Seb found so amusing.

"I was just thinking we're doing our bit for the environment." Seb kissed Ruther's leg again. "No need for wet wipes now."

Laughter rolled out of Rutger. He couldn't remember the last time he'd been as happy and contented as he was in that moment. Seb had more than lived up to the image Rutger had created of him over the six months of virtual contact. His laughter died on his lips. Before the day was out, they would be back to messages and videos.

Chapter Nine

"You weren't joking when you said you had sandwich toppings in your fridge." Seb stared at the collection of luncheon meats and cuts of cheese on display. He didn't have a clue as to what at least half of them were. He randomly picked something that didn't look like ham, put it on the slice of brown bread he'd just buttered, and took a bite. "Oh. Whatever this is, it's good."

Rutger gave him a bemused stare. "Did you think I'd serve you nasty food?"

"You know what I mean," Seb grumbled, too busy enjoying the large selection of new tastes to discover to come up with a more specific reply.

"I do," Rutger conceded. "I'm always amazed how limited the choice is in most other countries."

As they continued eating in silence, Seb studied the scene outside. As pretty as the still falling snow was, he was starting to worry about the sheer quantity of it. As soon as he'd eaten as much as he could—unfortunately without having been able to sample all the choices on offer—he turned to Rutger. "Should I be worried about getting to the airport?"

"I don't know." Rutger stared at his car. "I think we'll be fine as long as we can get the car safely from here to the main road. At least I live close to the exit and not on the far side." He focused on the outside world again and frowned. "I guess I'd better check my travel app, just in case." He patted his pocket. "I must have left my phone in the bedroom."

The moment Rutger stood, Seb heard the incoming message sound from his own phone. "I'll come with you."

His heart skipped a beat when he saw the text he'd received came from Aer Lingus. *This won't be good.* He'd checked himself in for the return flight as soon as he landed in Amsterdam, so it couldn't be a reminder.

We regret to inform you that all flights to and from Amsterdam have been canceled until further notice due to inclement weather. You can reschedule your flight on our website.

Fuck.

"Fuck." Rutger's exclamation coincided with Seb's.

"What?" they said at the same time.

"There's a countrywide no travel advisory," Rutger said. "Even if I can get the car to the main road, I don't think I can get you to the airport today."

Seb huffed out a frustrated laugh. "Don't worry about it. My flight has been canceled."

They looked at each other. The expression on Rutger's face implied that he hoped Seb had a solution to the situation.

Seb had a suspicion his features asked the same question.

"What do we do now?" Rutger asked. "I mean, you are more than welcome to stay here as long as you like." His features softened. "I don't mind having you here longer at all."

Despite the worry churning in his stomach, Seb filled with warmth. If it were just a matter of simply extending his visit, he wouldn't mind the current situation either.

"But you have a life you're supposed to return to," Rutger continued, reminding Seb that an awkward and almost certainly unpleasant phone call awaited him in the immediate future.

"There's not a whole lot I can do about it." Seb put more confidence in his voice than he felt. "Even my boss should be able to understand that this is an act of God rather than me being difficult." Seb chuckled. "Given how religious he proclaims to be, he should be very accepting of acts of God." He sobered again and stared at his phone. Was there any point in postponing the inevitable? Would his boss be more pissed off if Seb called today or tomorrow morning?

With a sigh, Seb scrolled through his contact list and pressed on the name he wanted. He might as well get it done and over with now. If he didn't, he'd spend the next day and night worrying about it.

"This had better be good, Seb. I don't like being

disturbed at home."

Off to a flying start.

"I'm sorry for calling you, Mr. Smith, but I've got a bit of a problem." Seb waited for a moment to see if that would trigger a reaction, but all he heard was silence. "I'm in the Netherlands, and I'm snowed in. There is no way I can make it back to Dublin to be in the office tomorrow."

"That's just not good enough. I don't care how you do it, but I fully expect to find you behind your desk tomorrow morning at nine. A little bit of snow is no excuse."

Seb stared through the bedroom window at the world outside where snow was still falling, and the wind had picked up so that snow drifts were starting to form. "It's quite a lot of snow actually. There's a national warning not to travel."

"Such warnings can be ignored in case of an emergency. You know that as well as I do." Mr. Smith now sounded both impatient and angry.

Struggling to hang on to a semblance of calm, Seb took a deep breath. "Even if I could make it to the airport, which I can't, Aer Lingus informed me that all flights have been canceled."

"I don't care. You may think it's not your fault you're snowed in, but it's even less mine. And it shouldn't be my problem." Mr. Smith sounded more pissed off by the second.

"You decided to get on a plane and put yourself in a situation where getting home on time might be difficult. If I'd known you were planning foreign travel, I wouldn't have given you the day off in the first place."

"But…" There was so much Seb wanted to say.

"Don't bother. It's simple. Either you're in the office tomorrow morning at nine, or you don't have to bother showing up at all."

"But…" Seb said again, but the connection had already been severed.

"Fuck. Fuck. Fuck." Seb threw the phone to the bed as fury and panic battled inside him.

"Seb? What happened?" Rutger took a step toward him, then stopped as if something about Seb had warned him not to proceed.

"What happened? You want to know what happened?" Seb knew he wasn't being reasonable but couldn't stop the anger from pouring out of him. "The bastard sacked me. Over the phone. For something I couldn't change if I wanted to. *That's* what happened.

Rutger stared at him wide-eyed. "Can he do that? Is that legal?"

"I don't know. Who cares? It's not as if I'm there to do anything about it, is it?" Seb listened to himself with increasing horror. Why was he lashing out at Rutger? But he couldn't stop himself. If he didn't allow his anger out, he might burst.

"Seb." Rutger raised his arms as if to embrace him, then lowered them again. "We'll figure it out. It will be okay."

"You're not fucking getting it." Rutger's platitudes fed Seb's rage. "I've just lost my job. Without my job, I'll lose my accommodation."

Rutger's eyes pleaded with Seb as he reached for him, but Seb was having none of it.

"Leave it." He turned on his heel and stalked to the front of the house. The fresh, thick layer of snow outside made opening the door hard, but Seb managed it. He stepped into the cold and walked off without bothering to close the door. He needed time to think. Surely there had to be a solution. As much as he detested his boss, he needed his job. He couldn't afford to be without a paycheck for even a week.

"Sebastian, wait!"

Seb ignored the call out, even though it was only the second time Rutger had used his full name. He was too furious. With himself. With his boss. With Rutger. And with the heavy clouds that continued to spill snow to a world that already had too much of it. Every time he took a step, his leg sank into the snow up to his calf. Cold water slowly soaked his trousers, then melted into his shoes.

It felt like he'd covered miles rather than less than fifty meters when Seb reached the bend in the road that would take him out of sight of the cottage. He glanced over his shoulder and noticed that the door remained wide open but that Rutger was nowhere to be seen. Relief and profound disappointment battled in Seb's heart. He needed to be alone right now, but it shattered him that apparently, Rutger didn't care enough to follow him.

He stumbled on through the snow until he spotted a pile of logs on his left. As much as Seb wanted to put distance between himself and Rutger and his perfect life, he couldn't go much farther. Walking through the snow was exhausting, and his feet were so cold he could barely feel them. He sat down on the top log and put his head in his hands.

What the fuck am I going to do now?

His eyes burned from the unfairness of it all. His first foreign break in over a year, and it had cost him his job. Was this the universe's way of telling him he wasn't supposed to have fun? Every single minute he'd spent with Rutger prior to that phone call had been perfect. He'd wasted energy planning future visits in his head. He'd even wished for a reason to stay longer, eejit that he was. Without a job, it wasn't as if he could afford to go anywhere. Provided that Rutger would still be speaking to him after his tantrum, of course.

Something brushed against his leg, startling Seb, and he

lowered his hands. Raeynar stood next to him with his head tilted. He sat and rested his snout on Seb's thigh.

"What are you doing here? Did you run away too?" He scratched Raey between his ears. "Did you come to remind me what a fool I am?"

Unsurprisingly, Raeynar said nothing, but his warm gaze didn't waver, and Seb could have sworn he saw understanding there.

"I probably won't see you again either. I'll miss you and your owner." A tear trickled down Seb's cheek, and he wiped it away angrily. As much as he hated the idea that he'd probably spoiled everything he and Rutger might have been, it was the least of his problems right now. For a moment he allowed the hope that the snow might disappear as suddenly as it had arrived to linger in his mind. Common sense reasserted itself immediately. Even if it did stop snowing that moment, the temperature would have to jump up by at least ten degrees for enough of it to melt to make travel possible again.

"Sweat Jaysus, what have I done?"

The forest didn't answer his question any more than Raeynar had, and its silence appeared to mock him. He'd literally burned all his bridges, and Seb had no idea how to fix them. He couldn't expect Rutger to put up with him any longer, not after the way Seb had lashed out and stormed off.

"There you are." Rutger's voice was soft and tinged with relief.

Seb refused to remove his hands from his face to look at Rutger. Shame and panic made for an uncomfortable combination as they raged through him.

"Here."

Something warm and heavy was draped over Seb's shoulders, and when he glanced through his fingers, he recognized his coat. As if the sight awakened his senses, Seb suddenly became aware of the cold that had seeped into his bones. When he felt Rutger's thigh press against his, Seb knew Rutger had joined him on the log pile.

"I understand that you're angry—"

Seb couldn't help himself and snorted.

"But things are rarely as bad as they seem at first glance," Rutger continued as if Seb hadn't interrupted him.

"How are you going to turn me losing my job and almost certainly also the room I rent into a positive?" Seb hated the bitter note in his voice. It wasn't who he normally was. Then again, he didn't normally lose his job so unexpectedly.

"Come back to the house, and we'll talk about it," Rutger said.

"What's there to talk about?" Seb's anger flared up again.

"Everything." Rutger sounded patient and kind. "Besides, we probably want to get you out of the cold before you get sick on top of everything else."

Because Seb couldn't argue with that, he allowed Rutger to take his hand and pull him up. When Rutger wrapped his gloved fingers around Seb's freezing hand, Seb fully understood how incredibly stupid he'd been when he'd flounced out of Rutger's cabin. He meekly followed Rutger back as the cold he'd been ignoring so far took hold of his body. By the time they were inside and Rutger had closed the door, Seb was shivering violently.

"Come." Rutger led the way into the living room, then pushed a chair in front of his stove, and pointed at it. "Sit."

Too emotionally drained to put up a fight, Seb did as instructed. Rutger knelt at his feet, and Seb wondered if maybe he had a fever and was hallucinating. When Rutger proceeded to remove Seb's shoes and socks, his actions made sense again, even if Seb had no idea why Rutger would want to show him such kindness after the way Seb had lashed out at him.

"Here's what we're going to do." Rutger took Seb's left foot in his hands and rubbed it. "You're staying here until the world has returned to normal. Longer if you want to."

A tingling sensation erupted in Seb's foot. It wasn't pleasant, and he almost pulled his foot free before he realized that it was probably his circulation kicking in again.

"Tomorrow, we're going online, and we'll investigate what your rights as an employee are. I don't know a lot about labor law, but I'm fairly sure sacking an employee isn't as easy as your boss seems to think." He lowered Seb's foot and picked up the second, now much colder one.

"I'm not sure it matters." Seb sighed. "Even if we find that he acted illegally, I can't see myself going back to work for him. Not after this." His anger had vanished to be replaced by a sense of hopelessness Seb wasn't sure how to penetrate or dismiss.

"You may still have rights. This looks to me like an unfair dismissal. You may be entitled to some sort of compensation."

Despite his despondency, Seb couldn't deny that Rutger might have a point. If nothing else, some sort of payment would mean he could meet his rent for a while longer.

"And there's nothing stopping you from looking and applying for jobs while you're here." Rutger released Seb's foot and placed his hands on Seb's knees. "We'll figure something out. Together. I promise."

Anger and fear still churned in Seb's stomach, and a large part of him wanted to surrender to those emotions. What was the point of trying to fight them? Believing Rutger's promise and embracing his optimism came with the distinct possibility of further disappointments.

Seb forced himself to look at Rutger, who still knelt at his feet. His beautiful, greyish-blue eyes were filled with compassion, understanding, and something else. It was difficult to hang on to his rage when Rutger's gaze seemed to promise him support and a smidgen of hope.

What do I have left to lose now?

His anger would always be there. He could fully embrace it when he was home again. His time with Rutger, on the other hand, was limited. The warmth Rutger had rubbed into Seb's feet seemed to have reached his heart, and a small spot of light pierced through the darkness.

Before Seb could react to Rutger's suggestions, his host's phone rang.

"*Verdomme.*" Rutger glared at the screen before sending Seb an apologetic look. "Sorry. It's my mother. I'd better take it. She'll just keep on calling if I don't."

"Sure." Seb didn't mind a little more time before he had to pull himself together. He couldn't stay in this funk indefinitely. Rutger had been nothing except kind, generous, and understanding. If Seb had to impose his presence on Rutger for longer than planned, being easy company was the least he could do.

Rutger's voice as he talked on the phone rumbled over Seb. None of the words made sense to Seb, so he studied Rutger's expressions, which went from a deep scowl via neutral to a tentative smile. Despite himself, Seb was curious what the conversation might be about, especially since Rutger threw an occasional glance Seb's way.

"Sorry about that," Rutger said after he ended the call. "Her timing could have been better."

The apologetic note in Rutger's voice brought an unexpected smile to Seb's face. "It's not as if she knows I just had a meltdown."

"You'd be surprised," Rutger mumbled. "Her call was about you and how we were dealing with being snowed in." He focused on Seb as if he wanted to figure something out. "She's invited us to dinner tonight if you're up for it."

Seb's immediate impulse was to say "hell no." Common sense kept his lips sealed until he'd reconsidered. Under the circumstances, he could do with all the distractions he could find.

"That sounds good."

Rutger's raised eyebrows told Seb he'd failed to convince him. "After all, I can't spend the rest of the day being miserable."

A sad but sweet smile played on Rutger's lips. "Go

ahead and be as miserable as you need. Raeynar and I will take care of you."

Seb leaned forward and rested his forehead against Rutger's. "I'm sorry for being a dick. Thank you for not being upset with me. It's more than I deserve."

Rutger placed his fingers under Seb's chin and lifted it. "Given the shock you've had, I think you're allowed to be a dick." He pressed his lips against Seb's for an undemanding, almost platonic kiss. "We'll figure it out."

Seb had no idea how they might do that but found himself believing Rutger and forced his mouth to form something that hopefully resembled a smile.

Raeynar got off his bed and joined them to lick Seb's hand.

If his life had to go to shit somewhere, maybe this cabin in the middle of nowhere in the Netherlands was the best place for it.

Chapter Ten

The forced grimace on Seb's face tore at Rutger's heart. Everything inside him yearned to make things better, to tell Seb he could stay forever, that Rutger would take care of him. Because it would be a ludicrous suggestion and would almost certainly enrage Seb, Rutger kept his thoughts and feelings to himself. Now was not the time to tell Seb that their two days together had confirmed what Rutger had known even before Seb arrived. He'd fallen for Seb while they connected online, and the past twenty-four hours had deepened that attraction. While it was obvious that Seb enjoyed being with him, Rutger didn't dare hope that Seb's feelings matched his.

Seb yawned, then shivered.

"Are you still cold?" Rutger checked the stove, which burned happily. It wasn't cold in his cabin, but Seb had been outside, without a coat, for long enough to have caught a chill.

"A bit," Seb admitted softly. "And exhausted." He winced. "I'm sorry. I must be the worst guest you've ever had."

"My worst. My best." Rutger chortled. "You're my first guest, so I can't compare."

"First?" For a moment, Seb looked like his old self, curious and fully engaged. "That's what your mother said too, but I thought she had to be wrong. Didn't you say you've lived here for five years?"

Rutger nodded. He hadn't planned on coming out as a near hermit, but under the circumstances, it might not be a bad thing.

"And you had no visitors in all that time?" Seb sounded incredulous.

"That's not what I said." Rutger fought the urge to get defensive. "You're the first person to stay for longer than a few hours. The first to stay the night."

Seb stared at him, and Rutger could easily imagine the questions running through his mind…Questions Rutger didn't want to answer. Not now. He pushed to his feet, took Seb's hand, and pulled him up. "Come. We've got hours before we have to fight the snow to get to my mother's place. We'll go back to bed and get you warm and rested."

When Seb followed him to the bedroom without a word, Rutger wasn't sure if it was a good or a bad sign. It was a relief that Seb was no longer upset with him, but he didn't like this meek version of the man he'd gotten to know as feisty and outspoken. Seb didn't show any initiative once they'd reached the bed either, so Rutger undressed him, making sure to keep the action free of touches that might be interpreted as seductive. He had no idea what Seb needed, but it probably wasn't sex.

"Lie down." Rutger pointed at the bed as soon as Seb was naked.

Still wordlessly, Seb complied, and Rutger tucked him in before placing a kiss on Seb's forehead and stepping back. "Try to sleep."

Seb looked up at him. "Stay with me?"

As if Rutger needed to be asked twice. He rounded the bed, shed his own clothes, and crawled under the covers too. Before he'd fully settled, Seb nestled against him, and Rutger wrapped his arm around him to pull him in closer.

"Thank you." Seb's mouth was pressed to Rutger's chest so that he felt the words more than heard them. "I don't want to be alone."

A bounce on the foot end of the bed announced Raeynar's arrival. Rutger followed the mutt's movements with his gaze and smiled when he curled up on the other side of Seb. Clearly, Rutger wasn't the only one determined to make sure Seb felt safe and cared for.

"You're not alone," Rutger murmured. "I'm here. I'll take care of you, I promise."

"I don't deserve it…you." Seb sounded drowsy.

"Nonsense." Rutger wanted to say so much more. He longed to tell Seb that he'd wished for a chance to keep Seb longer. If he could be sure that Seb would welcome the news,

Rutger would confess that he'd fallen for Seb and didn't want to say goodbye. Not today. Not tomorrow and ideally, not ever. Common sense told him that Seb had endured enough shocks for one day, so he kept his thoughts to himself as he listened to Seb's breathing becoming regular and deeper.

Sleep, my lad. Let me care for you. I'll keep you safe.

"Oh."

Rutger didn't know when he'd fallen asleep or how long he'd been out when wet warmth embracing his cock woke him. He opened his eyes, raised his head, and glanced down his body to discover that the covers had disappeared and a black mop of hair obscured his dick from view. He allowed his head to flop back to the pillow and took a few moments to simply enjoy Seb's mouth and tongue pleasuring him.

He would miss this too. The sex, of course, but the waking up together even more. How could he have gone from being perfectly happy on his own to dreading the moment he would be alone again in a day?

He placed his hand on Seb's head and combed his soft hair with his fingers. He needed the connection with Seb as much as he wanted to let Seb know he was awake. When Seb released his cock and looked at him, he almost regretted the action.

"Hey." Seb's smile was a little shy.

"What are you doing?" The stupidity of the question hit him as soon as Rutger asked it.

"What does it feel like?" Seb asked. While his question was humorous, his somewhat pinched expression told a different story. "Just relax and let me show you how grateful I am."

What?

Rutger sat up, grasped Seb's shoulder, and pulled until Seb faced him. "I don't need your gratitude. I didn't do anything." Rutger had no intention of allowing Seb to feel guilty or bad about what had happened, not on Rutger's behalf anyway.

Before Rutger finished his sentence, Seb lowered his head. *Verdomme.*

"Seb."

He didn't react.

"Seb, look at me, please."

The obvious reluctance with which Seb lifted his head tore at Rutger and made him want to kick himself. He would get his words right this time if it killed him.

"I love your mouth on my cock. It was magical the first time, and I have no doubt it will be just as good in the future."

The frown on Seb's face relaxed a little.

"In fact, if you want to give me a blow job, I'm all for it." Rutger winked and mentally crossed his fingers that his levity would have the desired effect.

The right corner of Seb's mouth lifted in a half smile.

"But don't do it unless it is what you want to do. You don't owe me anything, least of all gratitude. I didn't do anything because there's fuck all I can do."

"You could have gotten angry with me." Seb's voice was steady. "In fact, you probably should be upset with me. I had no business lashing out at you the way I did. I behaved like a brat and you…you." His voice broke.

Devastated, Rutger reached for Seb and pulled him close. "I did what every person who cares for you would have done. You were hurting, and I tried to help." A bitter laugh escaped him. "Not that I seem to be very successful."

The mattress bounced a little, and a moment later, Raeynar pressed his warm body against Seb's.

"Good doggo." Seb reached out and stroked Raeynar.

Rutger's heart melted. For reasons he didn't   quite understand, it was important that his dog and Seb were bonding. What was more, Raeynar appeared to be much better at comforting Seb than his owner was. Rutger rested his chin on Seb's hair and took advantage of the distraction Raey provided to work out what he wanted to say next.

"You don't have to apologize for getting angry." Rutger spoke over Seb's head. "You got a massive shock and reacted. I've lashed out in anger at people who didn't deserve it for worse reasons. It's just instinct taking over. I *know* your rage wasn't really aimed at me.

"It still doesn't feel right." Seb jutted out his jaw, and Rutger smiled at the mock defiance on his face. *That's better.*

"Then don't do it again." Without waiting for an answer, Rutger placed his fingers under Seb's chin, lifted it, and kissed him.

Within a heartbeat, Seb parted his lips and draped his arms around Rutger's neck. A deep sigh escaped Seb when their tongues connected. Rutger put everything he had into the kiss— every word that had failed him, every thought he hadn't been able to formulate, and every feeling he wasn't brave enough to voice. When they parted, they were both out of breath.

"Now if you want to blow me, be my guest." Rutger dropped back and made a show of his head bouncing when it landed on the cushion before he folded his hands behind his head and assumed a waiting position. He wasn't sure what it said about him that he'd stayed hard all through that conversation.

As if he knew exactly what was going on, Raeynar

jumped off the bed.

For a moment Seb didn't move and stared at him. Then his mouth stretched into a smile. "Don't mind if I do." He shuffled his way down the mattress on his knees and positioned himself between Rutger's spread legs. He licked his lips as he gazed at Rutger's crotch.

"I'm wait—"

When Seb inhaled Rutger's dick, not stopping until his nose touched Rutger's pubes, he thought he might have died and gone to heaven. *So good.* Seb sucked hard and teased with his tongue and drove Rutger out of his mind. Just as he thought Seb would blow him to one of his fastest orgasms ever, Seb slowed down and took his time teasing Rutger's cock with his tongue. The next time Rutger was sure he would come, Seb pulled back and licked Rutger's balls before lapping at them softly.

"You're killing me." *But what a way to die.*

Seb laughed around Rutger's cock, the vibrations adding yet another edge to the mind-blowing pleasure.

The moment Rutger thought he might be reduced to begging to come, Seb stopped teasing. His head bobbed, and his tongue swirled. Rutger closed his eyes as his balls tightened. His release started in his toes. He thrust up, and as Seb swallowed around the head of his cock, Rutger's orgasm slammed into him. Lights exploded behind his closed eyelids. *Heaven.*

Moments or maybe it was hours later, Rutger blindly reached for Seb and pulled him in for a kiss. Tasting himself on Seb's tongue satisfied Rutger in a different but equally amazing way. He stroked Seb's back, his hip, then moved his hand to Seb's groin.

"Not now." Seb gently took his wrist and pushed Rutger's hand back. "I don't care what you say. This was for you. Just because I happened to enjoy it doesn't make a difference." He grinned at Rutger. "Besides, we probably need to get ready to go to your mother."

Rutger sighed. Obviously, despite everything Rutger had said, Seb still believed he'd owed Rutger something. Rutger wanted to argue with Seb, convince him that he'd done nothing wrong. Doing so would almost certainly make the situation worse, so Rutger swallowed the words burning on his tongue. Since Seb wasn't going anywhere for the foreseeable future, Rutger would find his opportunity to return the favor.

Chapter Eleven

Seb *had* to pull himself together.

He stepped behind Rutger and followed him along the road, making use of what looked like a fresh tire track. Somebody had apparently been brave enough to drive through the deep snow.

Should Rutger have taken the risk?

Seb studied the track they were walking along and the one more than a meter to their right. They were too wide to have been made by a car. Seb was no expert, but these looked like they had been created by something like tractor tires. He laughed.

"What's so funny?" Rutger glanced at him over his shoulder before focusing on where he placed his feet again.

"I was imagining driving to the airport on a tractor."

"What?" Rutger stopped walking and turned.

Laughing, Seb pointed at the tracks. "Clearly, that's about the only mode of transport still functional."

Rutger stared at Seb, squinting a little. Then his brows lifted, and he laughed too…and continued laughing. As if his amusement stemmed from more than just Seb's silly joke. It probably did and all. Seb had been so busy focusing on his own misery he'd neglected to consider how his behavior might affect Rutger. Which was why Seb had to get his act together. He'd gone from lashing out at Rutger to becoming an emotional mess. It was a freaking miracle that Rutger still talked to him and, what was more, continued to show an interest in Seb.

They resumed their journey, and Seb's mind continued with its recriminations. Everything had been perfect until that phone call. Seb had had no doubts that they would continue to stay in touch, that more visits awaited in their futures. But now? He glanced at Rutger's back. Now he wouldn't blame Rutger if he cooled things off as soon as Seb went home. Seb wasn't sure why he hadn't already.

He hated it…himself. Rutger had been his hero before they'd connected online. He'd counted himself so lucky when they grew closer during their chats. The mutual attraction, their sexy videos. It had just gotten better and better. These two days were supposed to be the crown on the previous six months and, Seb had hoped, the beginning of something else, something more, something deeper. He kicked at the snow.

"Are you okay?" Rutger looked over his shoulder, frowning slightly.

"Yeah." Seb fought with himself. Unless he wanted to make things even worse than they already were, he had to snap out of his funk. He jumped to the side into the second track so that he could walk next to Rutger instead of behind him. "I'm just upset with myself for losing the plot so completely."

Rutger's expression was a mixture of resignation and regret. He held out his hand over the layer of snow between them and squeezed Seb's fingers as soon as their gloved hands were clasped.

"Maybe you should give yourself a break," Rutger said as he resumed walking. "You got a shock. You reacted." He shrugged, and the movement made their joined hands swing. "Don't turn it into a bigger drama than it is."

They arrived at a crossroad, and Rutger turned left. "Just a little bit farther."

It wasn't the first time Rutger had told Seb to stop worrying about how he'd reacted. It occurred to Seb that maybe he should pay attention to what Rutger said. After all, he had more than enough on his plate without adding fictional problems with Rutger to the equation.

They took a right turn, and Seb almost forgot to walk. He'd seen the house before but only now really noticed it. "That's no cabin." The building in front of him was a two-story, stone-built house. He guessed in Ireland they would call it country house-style. The front door sat between two large windows and had a small, roofed porch. Lights on the front wall, along the path leading up to the entrance, and blazing from the interior made the place appear welcoming and warm.

The front door opened before they reached it, as if Merel had been keeping an eye out for them. At the same time, Raeynar emerged from the trees into which he'd vanished as soon as they'd left Rutger's cabin. The dog shot past Merel into the house.

"There you are." Merel and Rutger did the three kisses thing, and Seb prepared himself for the same but instead found himself caught in a fierce embrace. "You poor boy. I can't believe you lost your job because you got caught up in this snowmergency."

"Snowmergency, Mam? Really?"

As Merel released him, Seb bit his tongue to stop himself from laughing when he saw the exasperated expression on Rutger's face.

"Why not?" Merel was undeterred. "We have snow, and it has created an emergency. Snowmergency is a good word, even if I probably made it up." She grinned at Rutger. "It's good to see I can still embarrass you, even if you're almost forty."

Rutger huffed out a breath and rolled his eyes at Seb but didn't say anything.

Seb liked what he saw. It was clear that Rutger and his mother had a great relationship, and Seb had been comfortable in Merel's company from the moment he'd met her. He followed her and Rutger into a room to the right of the front door. From outside, it had looked warm and inviting, and it more than lived up to the promise. A fire burned in a large hearth, and a couch and two comfortable-looking chairs stood in a half circle facing the blaze. Seb smiled when he spotted Raeynar, who'd secured himself a spot on a rug in front of the fire.

"Would you organize drinks for us, Rutger? I made some *glühwein*. It's in the kitchen." Before Rutger could answer her question, she turned to Seb. "Have a seat." She pointed at the couch.

"Some things never change," Rutger muttered good-naturedly before turning and leaving the room.

As soon as Seb and Merel sat, Merel studied him, her gaze suddenly serious. "Are you okay?"

Seb shrugged, unsure what to say. Obviously, he wasn't fine, but he didn't think it would help anybody if he went over the whole drama again. "It's a bit of a shock. I wasn't particularly happy in that job, but I wasn't ready to lose it yet. I would have preferred to wait until I have a new job lined up. But I guess it is what it is."

When he'd started his answer, he'd meant to reassure Merel. Now that he'd finished talking, he discovered that his words actually made a lot of sense. If only he'd come to the same conclusion a few hours earlier.

Rutger returned, carrying a tray holding three glass mugs filled to the brim with a red, steaming liquid. He placed the drinks on the table standing between the fireplace and the seats and sank onto the couch next to Seb. "I hope she hasn't been pestering you too?" His tone indicated his words were in jest.

"As if I would." Merel smiled at her son, then focused on Seb. "But if you get fed up staying with my son, you're always welcome here. I've got a wonderful spare bedroom upstairs."

Lost for words, Seb blinked at her. Was she serious? He couldn't escape the feeling that while she didn't for a second expect him to take her up on it, Merel would take him in without hesitation, should he ask.

"Are you okay, Mam?" Rutger's question saved Seb from having to come up with a reaction to Merel's offer. "According to the forecast, we've got at least four more days of snow ahead of us. Do you have everything you need?"

"I'm fine. Don't worry. But Cor came by this afternoon and told me that if any of us need anything, we can call him. He offered to take his tractor to the shop for us if necessary." She turned to Seb. "Cor is the farmer who owns the fields next to the estate." She indicated the back of her house with a wave of her hand.

"And nobody's run into trouble?" Rutger asked.

"Not as far as I know."

Merel and Rutger talked on, mentioning names that didn't mean anything to Seb. He allowed the words to flow over him while he sipped his drink and enjoyed the heat from the fire. He wasn't sure what he was drinking, but he liked it. Merel had called it *glühwein,* and while Seb had no idea what *glüh* meant, it certainly tasted like hot wine, probably with some added spices. It took him a while to realize that Rutger and Merel were speaking English because of him. He wondered if he should tell them that he wouldn't be offended if they spoke to each other in their own language but decided against it. If they were going out of their way to be polite and include him, it wouldn't do to seem ungrateful.

Raeynar left his spot in front of the heat and found a new position sitting next to Seb with his head on Seb's leg. Chuckling, Seb followed the silent but obvious request and scratched the dog between his ears.

"You like dogs, Seb?" Merel asked. "Are you owned by a dog too?"

Three hours later, Rutger, Seb, and Raeynar carefully made their way back to Rutger's cabin. To Seb's mind, living in a forest was all well and good, idyllic even, but only during the day. Right now, he really missed street lights. The tractor tracks had all but disappeared thanks to a load of fresh snow, and it was impossible to see where it might be safe to put his feet.

As if to prove a point, his left foot hit an icy patch, and Seb had to work his arms to keep his balance. His movements were so wild he managed to hit Rutger.

"Careful." Rutger grabbed Seb's waving hand and steadied him.

"Yeah." Seb grimaced. "It's a bit slippery around here."

"It is?" Rutger laughed. "Wow. I hadn't noticed. I wonder if it's anything to do with all that white stuff."

"Ha. Ha. Very funny, you bollix." Seb tried to sound affronted, but he couldn't keep it up. His lips twitched, and he burst out laughing too.

When they started walking again, Rutger didn't let go of Seb's hand. Seb had no idea if that was because he wanted to make sure Seb didn't fall or because he enjoyed the contact, but he hoped it was a little of both.

They walked in silence for a while. Raeynar skipped in and out of the forest as if making sure they were still there before following a fascinating new scent.

Seb breathed out a sigh of utter contentment. It had been a good, no, a wonderful evening. Merel had been delightful and comfortable company. Unlike Seb's mother, she didn't suffer from the need to be fussy. Much to his relief, nobody had mentioned his predicament after Merel's initial remarks. Instead, they'd talked about life in the forest as opposed to life in Dublin and a whole host of other interesting but not overly personal subjects. He hadn't known it before the visit, but this evening had been exactly what he'd needed.

They passed the pile of logs where Seb had found refuge that morning. It was now mostly obscured, as if the fresh snow covering it was hiding the evidence of Seb's idiocy. He glanced beyond the logs and stopped walking.

"That's fabulous." Seb stared in awe at the clearing, where the full moon lit up the snow and turned the surrounding trees into almost menacing shadows. When a dark shape emerged from the trees and ran across the glade, Seb's heart skipped a beat. He chuckled when he realized his monster was in fact Raeynar.

Rutger stood behind him, wrapped his arms around Seb's middle, and rested his chin on Seb's shoulder. "It's gorgeous, all right. Just not very practical when you need to go places."

Seb chuckled. "Tell me about it." He stilled. This was the first time he could talk about the whole mess without feeling as if his life had ended.

"I'm sorry about your job." Rutger's voice was barely a whisper, and his mouth was so close to Seb's ear that warm air blew across it as Rutger spoke. "But I can't be sorry that I get to keep you a while longer."

Seb relaxed into Rutger's hold and sighed. "Staying longer doesn't bother me either. Two days never felt like long enough. If it wasn't for the whole 'I lost my job and can't afford to waste time before finding something else' business, I'd be over the moon that I don't have to go back yet."

"You mean that?" Rutger spun Seb around so that they faced each other.

The moonlight made Rutger's eyes darker, almost smoldering. It also gave his hair highlights, and the overall result took Seb's breath away. Suddenly and inexplicably a little shy, he nodded.

Rutger cupped Seb's nape and kissed him. Except that it was more than a kiss. The way Rutger's lips pressed against Seb's, combined with Rutger's tongue urging its way into Seb's mouth, felt like a statement, a claiming even. Seb's heart soared. He didn't know what it meant and had even less of an idea as to what they would—could—do with it in the future. For now, that didn't matter. For now, he was happy that he hadn't alienated Rutger, that Rutger appeared to want him as much as Seb wanted Rutger.

A large part of Seb's life might be a mess, but at least he hadn't fucked up everything…especially this. Whatever *this* was.

Chapter Twelve

Rutger closed his book and rested his head against the couch cushion. *I could get used to this.* It was a bit of a revelation. Up until a few days ago, he would have described himself as a workaholic. Heck, he'd first adopted Raey because having a dog would force him to take breaks and go outside for walks. Yet here he was, lounging on the couch with his feet on the coffee table, reading a book he'd owned for months but never opened.

He glanced down at Seb, who had stretched out across the rest of the couch while using Rutger's thigh as a pillow. And there was the reason for Rutger's newly discovered contentment.

"I can feel you looking at me." Seb looked up and caught Rutger's gaze. "Did you finish your book?"

"No. I've got another thirty pages or so. I was thinking about a cup of coffee." That hadn't been on Rutger's mind at all, but now that he'd mentioned it, he discovered he wanted one. He straightened.

"I'll get it." Seb placed his Kindle on the couch, swung his legs to the floor, and stood. "It's my turn." He bent forward to kiss Rutger before walking to the kitchen.

That there was another reason for Rutger's serenity.

Apart from the "lost-job incident," as they now called it, everything and every moment with Seb had been easy and comfortable. They'd known they shared interests, tastes, and hobbies before they'd met at the airport. From the moment they arrived at the cabin, it had been obvious that physically they might well have been made for each other. Their desires were perfectly matched, and they seemed to intuit what the other needed or wanted.

He listened to Seb singing softly in the kitchen. He didn't know the song, something about an ordinary man, but he loved the sound of Seb's voice. It wasn't the only thing he loved about Seb either. Seb had slotted into Rutger's life in a matter of days. He refused to be a guest and demanded his equal share in whatever needed to be done. He'd arrived four days ago, but already Rutger couldn't help feeling Seb belonged here.

A soft whistle sounded from the kitchen, and Raeynar, who lay on his bed near the stove, lifted his head, his ears pricked before he got up and trotted to the kitchen, where Seb would no doubt be handing him a treat. Rutger smiled. He should have known he'd picked a winner when Raey had taken a shine to Seb right from the start.

Rutger sobered. That winner would have to go back home in the not-too-distant future. The weather forecast predicted a further three days of snow and freezing temperatures before a thaw would set in. Even if he gave it another two days for the snow to melt, Seb would only have been with him for ten days.

The patter of dog nails on the hardboard floor pulled Rutger out of his thoughts. Seb, wearing socks, moved silently, but Raeynar didn't have that advantage. The dog was clearly excited and stuck close to Seb. Rutger had a suspicion there might be a second treat on the tray Seb was carrying. Raeynar was being spoiled rotten and loving every moment of it.

As soon as he sat next to Rutger, Seb pulled his phone from his pocket. "I guess I'd better check my emails."

The resigned note in Seb's voice tore at Rutger. Seb had spent two days polishing his résumé and sending it off, as well as updating his LinkedIn profile and putting out feelers there. Rutger had been tempted to offer him help, and he'd been close to checking him out on LinkedIn, but he'd refrained. If Seb wanted his assistance, he'd ask. It wouldn't do to intrude, but it had killed him to see Seb's despondency increase over the past few days.

"Anything?" Rutger asked the question, although the frown on Seb's face told him everything he needed to know.

"Sweet f-all." Seb put his mobile away. "I don't know why I'm surprised. January isn't a good month to go job hunting. Most companies are just back after being closed for a week. It's going to take time, and that's the one thing I don't really have."

Unsure what to say, Rutger placed his hand on Seb's thigh and squeezed.

"There I go again." Seb sent Rutger a half smile. "Don't mind me. It will probably all work out in the end. I'm not going to let my lack of success so far ruin the rest of my time here."

"You're allowed to worry, you know." Rutger was touched that Seb seemed determined to stay upbeat, but it wasn't necessary.

"I do know that." Seb sounded half-surprised. "But it's not going to help, and I'd just as soon feel good while I'm here." He grinned at Rutger. "Feel like playing a game?"

"What game?" As if Rutger had to ask.

"*Raeynar's Realm* of course." Seb grinned. "I'm going to find a way to beat the man who created that gem sooner or later."

Laughter bubbled out of Rutger. They'd played the game for at least an hour or two every day. Seb seemed obsessed with the idea of beating Rutger. Since Rutger knew every trick in the book—because he'd thought up every single one of them—Seb's chances were slim to none. Having said that, Rutger couldn't deny that Seb had a very good understanding of the game, almost as if he could see beyond the screen into the coding behind it.

"Sure." He took a last sip of his coffee. "Set it up."

Less than a minute later, they sat next to each other, leaning toward the large screen on the opposite wall with controllers in their hands. Seb's avatar, an elven figure with long, raven-black hair, appeared.

Not for the first time, Rutger marveled at how much it resembled Seb. Apart from the long hair and the pointy ears, it could almost be a photo of Seb, although he hadn't met Seb until four years after he'd created the character. Rutger pressed a few buttons on his controller and was ready to call up his own avatar when his phone rang.

"Sorry." He extracted his mobile and checked the screen. Anita? What did she want?

A few days earlier, Rutger had taken a for him uncharacteristic decision and informed the three game designers working for him that he would be taking extra time off. He had added that they should only contact him in case of an emergency. He really didn't need an emergency now.

Rutger connected the call and brought his phone to his ear. "Anita. What's wrong?"

"I can't get the code in this one section of the game to work properly. It doesn't matter what I try. It won't load two of the options we created. It's during the final section too, so we really need them."

Verdomme. That was bad. The game was supposed to be finished. It was scheduled to go to beta game testers in a week.

"I know you're on a break," Anita continued when she didn't get a response from Rutger. "But could you have a look? I really don't know what else to try. I've talked to Bert and Frank, but they can't figure it out either."

As if he had a choice. Owning a business came with responsibilities, convenient or not. "I'll check it out now. You keep at it too. We'll figure it out."

"What's wrong?" Seb asked as soon as Rutger ended the call.

Rutger decided to downplay the issue. There was no need for Seb to know how potentially disastrous it would be if it turned out to be more than a minor problem. "We appear to have run into a snag in the new game."

"A new game?" Seb's eyes lit up. "Why didn't you tell me there's a new game coming?"

The obvious excitement in Seb's voice warmed Rutger. He shrugged. "I'm on a short break. I didn't want to think or talk about work." It wasn't the entire truth. The briefness of Seb's visit had been Rutger's original reason for staying quiet. And since Seb's misfortune, Rutger had avoided all talk about jobs unless Seb brought it up.

"What's the problem?" Seb asked, their game still paused on the screen, apparently forgotten.

"I won't know for sure until I look, but according to one of my designers, it won't load two options near the end. And we're running out of time. I've got testers lined up less than a week from now." Rutger was both relieved and impressed that he managed to sound unconcerned.

Seb opened his mouth, then closed it again and looked away. "You'd better go and do your thing then."

Rutger was convinced that Seb had initially wanted to say something else. His curiosity spiked, but he pushed it away. He'd ask about it later. He really needed to get to his office.

"I'm sorry." Rutger stood. "These few days were supposed to be all about you."

A genuine and bright smile lit up Seb's face. "Don't apologize. It's not as if you could have foreseen this happening." His smile turned into a smirk. "Besides, if your new game is anything near as good as this one"—he inclined his head toward the screen—"I can't wait to play it, so you'd better figure it out."

"I'll be as fast as I can." Rutger kissed Seb. "We'll play later."

Seb wrapped his arms around Rutger's neck and

claimed another kiss. "Don't hurry on my account. Just get it fixed."

In his office, Rutger powered up his computers, logged into the account he shared with his coworkers, and brought up the game's engine, focusing specifically on the lines flagged by Anita. He didn't dive straight into debugging, though, as his mind still marveled about how easy and understanding Seb had been. Rutger's last boyfriend had left him because he hadn't been able to put up with Rutger investing virtually every waking moment in the creation of his first game and establishing his company. Rutger hadn't been looking for more proof that Seb was as close to a perfect match for him as any man could be, but he guessed he'd found it anyway.

With a sigh, he focused on his monitors. At first glance, he couldn't see a reason why the two options wouldn't load. Everything seemed to be perfect. But as he ran the game through again, he saw that Anita had been right. Two of the variables were missing from the choices offered to the player.

As Rutger made minor tweaks, he chatted with Bert, Frank, and Anita, and ran other variations, then gradually lost track of time. It was infuriating. He was certain this hadn't been an issue the last time he'd worked on the game. What had happened? Checking older versions of the code didn't provide any answers either, and Rutger wanted to pull his hair out.

"Godverdomme." For the first time since he'd started his career six years earlier, Rutger wanted to take his computers and chuck them out the window.

"Are you okay?" Seb stood on the threshold of the office. The frown lines on his forehead betrayed his concern.

"No!" Rutger took a deep breath and tried again. "Something is wrong, but I can't find where exactly or why."

Seb pushed away from the doorway and approached him. When he stood behind him, Seb placed his hands on Rutger's shoulders and squeezed softly. "May I have a look?"

"Sure." Rutger didn't understand the question; to the uninitiated, the information on his screen wouldn't mean anything. Since he didn't have the mental energy to also solve the mystery of Seb's show of interest, he let it go.

A moment later, Seb had pushed a chair next to Rutger's and sat squinting at the screen. "That's clever," he murmured, followed by "how does that work?" and "ah, now I see it."

Rutger switched his attention from the screens to Seb, whose statements amazed him. Clearly, Seb's knowledge about games extended beyond playing them. A wide variety of expressions flashed across Seb's features, and Rutger thought he recognized delight and awe, all caught up in total concentration.

"So, where does it all go wrong?" Seb asked eventually.

"There." Rutger pointed at a section of lines on one of the monitor screens.

Without asking if it was okay, Seb took control of Rutger's mouse and scrolled back through the code. He started muttering again, but Rutger didn't recognize any words.

"There," Seb said after what felt like a lifetime. "What's happening here?" He highlighted a section of the screen.

Rutger studied the code Seb had indicated and opened his mouth to explain the succession of commands when he suddenly understood Seb's question. That was the answer, wasn't it? So simple now that Seb had found it, and so easy to fix.

"What the fuck? How did we miss that?" Rutger wanted to hit himself.

"May I?" Seb asked again.

"Work away. I made a backup the moment I logged in." Rutger had a long list of questions for Seb, but they could wait until after this crisis had been resolved. He leaned back in his chair and watched as Seb took over his keyboard and made a few minute changes before scrolling back through to where Rutger had thought the problem lay.

"That should do it," Seb said without taking his eyes off the screen. "Let's run it."

A mere second after the game performed exactly as it should—with the inclusion of the two errant variables—Rutger's phone chimed again.

"I guess that's why you're the boss." Anita's voice was laden with relief and delight. "I was watching you work and had no idea what you were doing until it all came together."

Rutger chuckled. "That wasn't me."

"Uh? According to the information on my screen, that was you making those changes."

"I'll explain later," Rutger said. "It was my computer all right. It just wasn't me who fixed the problem." His subsequent laughter was pure delight rather than humor.

As soon as he ended the call, Rutger turned to Seb. "Thank you." He pulled him close, cradled Seb's face, and pressed their lips together. He poured all his relief into the kiss, mostly because he didn't have the words to express his gratitude. When they eventually pulled apart, he studied Seb. "When you said you'd do just about anything to have my job, I thought it was a manner of speech or a reference to a childhood fantasy you never got to fulfill." He gave Seb a hard stare. "I think you owe me an explanation."

Chapter Thirteen

Seb was still trying to catch his breath after the intense kiss when Rutger's words sank in. He'd had no intention of sharing that particular dream of his with Rutger, but apparently, keeping quiet was no longer an option.

"What do you want to know?" Seb was pretty sure he knew the answer to his question, but it bought him another moment before he had to come clean.

"How did you do that?" Rutger pointed at the screens. "How did you know where to look?"

"It's what I studied. I've got a qualification in computer science and video game design." Seb didn't elaborate. He didn't need to be a mind reader to predict how Rutger would react to his confession.

"I should have known," Rutger said under his breath. He turned to Seb. "Just before Anita called, I thought that you played the game as if you could see beyond the visuals to what lay beneath them. I can't believe I didn't work it out earlier."

It wasn't the reaction Seb had expected, and he relaxed a little. "I had no intention of telling you," Seb said honestly. "You weren't supposed to notice that I was more than an enthusiastic fan either."

"Why the hell not?" Rutger looked surprised and maybe a little frustrated.

"I didn't want you to think I only chatted with you because of who you were, because I hoped to get something out of the friendship we were developing."

They'd only been a few weeks into their online chatting when Seb had discovered who Rutger was. He'd thought long and hard about telling Rutger that he was living and working Seb's dream. They'd been in the early stages of what Seb had hoped would turn into a real friendship, and he didn't want Rutger to think that Seb's interest was related to Rutger's standing in the gaming world.

"Okay." Rutger nodded as if Seb's words made perfect sense to him. "I guess I understand that."

Seb breathed a sigh of relief. It wasn't that he regretted the decision he'd made back then, but he couldn't deny that he'd withheld information about a large part of himself, and it was good to know Rutger didn't hold it against him.

"But what about now?" Rutger asked. "Why didn't you say something after you lost your job?"

"And make it sound as if I expected you to solve my problem?" If anything, Seb had become more determined to keep his qualifications a secret after that disastrous phone call.

"What jobs did you apply for?" Without waiting for an

answer, Rutger turned to his computer and opened a fresh browser window.

Seb's heart sank when he saw Rutger open LinkedIn and bring up Seb's name.

"I knew I should have checked," Rutger muttered to himself as he studied Seb's profile.

With his heart in his throat, Seb watched as Rutger scrolled through his details. He focused on Rutger's face since he knew exactly what was visible on the screen.

"Did you at least apply for jobs with game designers?" Rutger asked after what felt like a lifetime to Seb.

"Open applications. Sure." Seb routinely sent out feelers to such companies. The process was a major frustration in his life. "It never leads to anything, though. Internships are easy enough to get, but I can't afford to work for nothing. I'm never considered for paying jobs because I lack practical experience." He shrugged. "Without experience, I can't get a job, and without a job, I can't get the required experience."

"I don't believe this." Rutger sounded frustrated.

"What?" Seb froze. Had his secrecy achieved what his outburst had failed to do and ruined his growing relationship with Rutger? *Please. No.* Things had been perfect in the past few days. They'd lived together as if they'd been in a relationship for years rather than less than a week. Seb didn't think he'd ever forgive himself if he'd wrecked that connection.

"I really wish you'd told me." Rutger opened yet another tab to a site Seb recognized as belonging to Rutger's company. "Look." Rutger pointed at the screen.

The headline on the page said "vacancy." Seb read on, then read the relatively short text again.

"You're looking for a game designer? Are you expanding?" Seb's heart rate increased, but he refused to follow the direction of thoughts his brain wanted him to take. Things like that didn't happen, not in real life, not for Seb.

Rutger chuckled. "I *was* looking for a designer."

"You found someone. Congratulations." Seb tried to sound cheerful for Rutger but couldn't help the stab of disappointment. Despite his best attempts to not get his hopes up, the news hit him hard.

Rutger's face was a blank canvas as he stared at Seb without saying a word.

"What?" Rutger's unblinking stare unnerved Seb.

"When can you start?" Rutger's mask fell away, and he grinned at Seb.

"What?" Seb felt like a fool as he stared openmouthed at Rutger and hoped the second shoe would drop soon.

Without speaking, Rutger reached for Seb and captured his mouth in a blistering kiss, taking full advantage of Seb's parted lips.

Seb surrendered. His mind couldn't keep up. His thoughts swirled around in his head so fast he couldn't get a grip on them. Did Rutger really just offer him a job, or had he misunderstood? Was he even awake? Surely this was a dream? He concentrated on the familiarity of the kiss, on Rutger's taste, and on the heat their encounter created in his veins. When Rutger pulled back, a small moan escaped Seb.

"Well?" Rutger gave him an expectant stare. "Will you come and work for me?"

"Just like that?" Seb whispered. "No formal interview? No checking my references and abilities?"

Rutger stared at him as if he'd grown a second head. "Formal interviews are to get to know a candidate, and I think we're past that stage. You've just fixed a problem I and my coworkers couldn't get our heads around." Rutger shook his head as if he still couldn't believe it. "I think that establishes your abilities, don't you?"

All Seb could do was nod. He didn't trust his voice to be steady if he tried to speak.

"As for references"—Rutger winked—"I think we both know what your former employer would say if I were to contact him." Rutger laughed. "The man's a fool for allowing so much talent to slip through his fingers, but I'm not complaining. His loss is most definitely my gain." Rutger narrowed his eyes. "Unless you have a criminal record you haven't mentioned or a history as a hacker, I think we're good." His lips twitched.

It was really happening. A dream Seb hadn't been brave enough to entertain was coming true.

"Well, what do you say? Can I take this message down or what?"

Everything in Seb screamed at him to just say yes, but he held back. He had a few more questions first.

"Where would I live?" He couldn't be sure, but Seb had a feeling finding accommodation in the Netherlands might be as difficult as it was in Ireland.

"Here, of course." Rutger's tone of voice made it clear that Seb's future address had never been in question. "And if moving in with me is too much, too soon, you can always take my mother up on her offer." He laughed again.

"And what about us?" It was Seb's last and probably his most important query. No matter how much he wanted the job, he wanted to hang on to Rutger even more.

"What about us?" Rutger frowned as if he didn't understand what had inspired Seb's question.

"You would be my boss. Wouldn't that complicate things? How are your other employees going to feel about the latest addition to the team sleeping with the owner of the company?"

"I hope you'll be a bit more than just my fuck buddy." Rutger smirked but quickly sobered when Seb didn't relax. "Right now, I think you're probably their favorite person in the entire universe," Rutger continued. "And unless I'm very mistaken, they're not the sort of people to worry about our relationship as long as it doesn't interfere with the job at hand." He reached for Seb's hands. "Just say yes. We'll figure out the practicalities later."

"Yes."

A smile stretching almost from ear to ear erupted on Rutger's face.

"And just so you know," Seb continued. "As much as I like your mother, I think I prefer to live with her son."

"I'm very glad to hear it." Rutger pulled at Seb's hands until he stood, then nodded at his lap.

Delighted to oblige, Seb sat and pushed in close. He had a feeling it hadn't been Rutger's main concern when he bought his office chairs, but Seb appreciated the lack of armrests. It made snuggling up so much easier. He rested his hand against Rutger's cheek and brushed his fingers through the soft hair of Rutger's beard.

Rutger slipped his hands underneath Seb's sweater and stroked his back. "I can't believe I won't have to give up on this.

I was planning trips to Dublin in my head. The moment I saw you in the arrivals hall, I knew saying goodbye to you would be devasting."

"Me too," Seb admitted as he combed the fingers of his other hand through Rutger's hair. "I almost told you too."

"Why didn't you?"

"Because I didn't think it served a purpose. I wasn't sure how you felt about me, but I figured that even if your feelings matched mine, there wasn't a whole lot either of us could do about the fact that we live in different countries."

"Lived." Rutger's eyes sparkled. "We won't be a flight away from each other for much longer."

Seb didn't want to talk about the practicalities of moving country right then. He wanted something a lot more intimate. He leaned in and traced kisses from the corner of Rutger's mouth to his ear before whispering, "I want you."

"Yes!" The word was almost a growl as Rutger straightened in his chair before he grabbed Seb's arse cheeks and picked him up as he stood.

"Color me impressed." Seb heard the breathless quality in his own voice but thought he had an excuse. It wasn't everyday somebody lifted him, never mind from a sitting position. It was hot and exhilarating all at the same time.

A few moments later, as Seb knelt on the bed and

presented his naked arse to Rutger, the heat went up a few notches. When Rutger's cock breached him, Seb sighed. *Perfection.* The stretch, the minor burn, and the sensation of Rutger entering…claiming him, combined with the knowledge that he wouldn't have to give up on Rutger or the way they fit together so perfectly was almost more than he could take. Tears gathered in his eyes, and he was glad Rutger couldn't see his face. He couldn't make sense of the sudden rush of emotion himself.

Rutger wrapped his fingers around Seb's dick. As he pumped in and out of Seb's hole, he pushed Seb's cock through his lube-slicked hand.

This would be short but oh-so sweet, and Seb didn't mind. There would be endless opportunities for leisurely intercourse, wild sex, or imaginative games. Right now, all he wanted was this closeness.

Rutger draped his upper body over Seb's back and kissed his nape. "I'm close," he warned.

"Me too." Seb's balls grew heavy, and his muscles tensed as his release built. "Don't stop. Harder."

"Pushy much," Rutger grunted, but he complied instantly.

Wave after wave of undiluted pleasure washed over Seb until he wasn't sure where he ended and Rutger began. Rutger hit Seb's prostate, and the electrifying pleasure triggered Seb's orgasm. It started in his toes and took hold of his body. His muscles locked, and his skin tingled as spurt after spurt of cum pulsed over Rutger's hand and onto the bedcovers.

"So tight. So good." Rutger used both hands to hold Seb in place as his cock expanded deep inside Seb. "You. Are. Everything. I. Never. Knew. I. Needed." Rutger's words came in a staccato rhythm.

Seb was too lost in the afterglow to respond, but he couldn't agree more. When he'd arrived in the Netherlands, he'd hoped to enjoy himself for two days. He'd looked forward to fun and games, both in bed and on the console. Not in his wildest dreams had he imagined that he might end up playing—and winning—for love.

Epilogue

New Year's Morning a year later

"Thanks." Merel smiled at Rutger and Seb. "That was a great night."

"Yeah, it was good," Bert chimed in while Anita and Frank nodded.

"It was our pleasure," Seb said before Rutger could react. "It's a shame we couldn't have the bonfire this year, but I enjoyed this."

Rutger glanced at the window. The rain was still hammering down, as it had for the past twelve hours or so, and a strong wind howled around the house. Inviting his mother and his employees over for a get-together in his—no, their—cabin had been a last-minute idea, but it had worked out just fine.

It was half past one now. The New Year had started, and their guests were supposed to be leaving. Except that they appeared reluctant to brave the elements, although Frank's car was parked almost up against the front door.

"I still think getting those board games out was an inspired idea," Anita said. "I'd forgotten how much I enjoy them. Everything I play appears to come with a screen these days."

"We could make it a regular thing," Seb suggested.

"Games night. Sounds good." Bert grinned, then turned to the door. "I guess we'd better do this."

As soon as the door opened, a blast of wet and cold air hit them. Moments later, the four guests had rushed to the car. Rutger was about to close the door when he reconsidered.

"Raeynar."

With great reluctance, the dog got up from his bed and approached the door. He stuck his nose out, then retreated two steps.

"Smart dog," Seb muttered.

Rutger couldn't argue more, but that didn't change the fact that Raey needed to go out before they went to bed. "Go on, boy."

Slinking low on his legs, Raeynar walked past them and into the rain. The moment he was outside, his demeanor changed, and he raced off. Less than a minute later, he returned and extracted his revenge when he shook of the water as soon as he stood next to Rutger before going back to his bed.

"Poor doggo." Seb chuckled as he crossed the room. He picked Raeynar's towel from the clothes dryer and rubbed the dog. "Your master's a cruel man, isn't he?"

Rutger snorted. "Would you have been happy to get up to let him out at six in the morning?"

"I guess not." Seb straightened. "But I don't mind Raeynar thinking I'm the good guy in this house." He walked to Rutger and wrapped his arms around his neck. "You're such a harsh taskmaster, boss."

"I noticed." Rutger pulled Seb closer. "You've been bribing him since the day you arrived."

"Three-hundred-and-sixty-six days ago." Seb kissed Rutger. "And there are moments it still feels like a dream."

Dreamlike was a good description. Miraculous worked too. Of course, there'd been a few less than glorious moments, but overall, their time together had been more and better than Rutger could have hoped for. In the end, Seb had only returned to Dublin for a long weekend. Rutger had gone with him to help him pack and to meet Seb's family. He chuckled.

"What?" Seb asked, although his eyes were already sparkling.

"I was thinking about when I met your family. You'd warned me your mother would give me the third degree, but nothing could have prepared me for that onslaught."

Seb laughed. "Irish mammies." He stilled and gazed at Rutger. "You impressed her. She loves you now." He kissed Rutger again. "Not as much as I love you, though."

Rutger sank into the kiss and brushed his tongue across Seb's lips. Seb opened up to him instantly, and their kiss deepened. A year after the first time, Seb's mouth was still as tempting and as tasty as it had been then. Rutger had assumed their passion would lose some of its urgency and glamor as time went by, but he was very happy to concede he'd been wrong. The first tingles of lust spread through his veins, and Rutger grabbed Seb's arse as an all too familiar hunger roused him.

"Not yet." Seb stepped back with an apologetic smile on his face. "I've got something to give you."

Fuck. "Me too." Rutger wasn't sure how he'd managed to forget.

"Mine's in the bedroom," Seb said.

"You go ahead. I'll follow you with mine." Rutger's heart rate increased. He thought it was a good idea, one of the best ideas he'd ever had, in fact. He just wasn't sure how Seb might react.

He watched Seb for a moment as he walked to the bedroom and admired that tight arse in the even tighter jeans. He pulled himself together. There would be time for that backside later. First things first... He retrieved the envelope from the drawer in his wall unit and followed Seb, mentally crossing his fingers that he was doing the right thing.

Seb sat in the middle of their bed, still fully dressed. Rutger wasn't sure whether to be relieved or disappointed that Seb hadn't stripped, but didn't say a word as he positioned himself opposite Seb.

"Here." They each held out their right hand at the same time.

When they laughed, they both sounded nervous.

"Take this first." Rutger shook the hand in which he held the envelope. "Please."

Seb glanced at his own hand, and Rutger followed his gaze. His breathing stuttered when he saw the small purple box Seb held. His curiosity spiked, and he cursed himself for being so hasty.

"Sure." Seb took the envelope, opened it, and extracted the documents inside. He glanced over the first page and the second before frowning at Rutger and studying the first one again. "What am I looking at?"

"What does it look like?" Rutger asked with his heart in his throat.

"It looks as if you're giving me half your company." Seb's frown deepened. "But that can't be right."

"That's exactly what it is," Rutger whispered because he didn't trust his voice. "If you sign your name next to mine, Regtur Games will be ours instead of mine."

The silence that settled in the room felt heavy. Seb stared at the papers in his hand, and Rutger couldn't read his expression because Seb had bowed his neck. What if he'd made a mistake? What if this was too much, too soon for Seb?

"Why would you do that?" Seb's wide-eyed gaze held wonder. "You created that company. You made it a success. I'm just somebody who joined your crew after you'd made your name."

"You're not *just* anything." The fierceness in his own voice surprised Rutger. "You are my world. You've given me everything I never knew I needed. I know it sounds like romantic claptrap, but you completed my life." Rutger swallowed. They'd professed their love for each other at least a thousand times over the past year, but this felt bigger. "If I had to choose between you and the company, I'd choose you. In a heartbeat and without a doubt." It took every ounce of courage he had, but Rutger forced himself not to avert his gaze from Seb's face.

"Oh." Seb swallowed visibly, and his eyes were a bit watery. "Oh." He glanced at his left hand in which he still clutched the purple box. A small smile tugged at his lips. "I guess I timed this just right, then." He held out his gift.

With shaking hands, Rutger took the box. Nerves swirled through his stomach, and his heart raced. He lifted the lid and stared at two rings. The center was formed by a crowned heart, held by two hands stretched into a rainbow-striped band.

"Before you get any ideas," Seb said, sounding as

nervous as Rutger felt. "This is not a marriage proposal."

Confused, Rutger studied Seb's face.

"I mean, I'd marry you without a second thought, but that's not what those rings are about."

A warm glow spread from Rutger's heart through his body. Marriage had never crossed his mind, so he wasn't sure why he'd felt a stab of disappointment when Seb said he wasn't proposing.

"What are they about, then?" Rutger pulled one ring from the black velvet display cushion and studied it.

"It's called a Claddagh ring," Seb said. "The heart stands for love, the hands for friendship, and the crown for loyalty. Tradition says that if you wear it with the heart pointed toward your wrist, you're taken because you've given your heart to someone else." Seb took the second ring and pushed it down the ring finger on his right hand with the heart pointing toward his wrist.

Much to his surprise, Rutger's eyes stung as he stared at Seb's finger. He didn't need a proposal if he held Seb's heart. Just as Seb held his. He copied Seb's movements, making sure the heart pointed the right way as he pushed it down his ring finger.

He reached for Seb and toppled both of them over as soon as he held him. Seb laughed as Rutger pulled him close.

They'd have to undress and otherwise get ready for bed, but not yet. For now, Rutger just wanted to hold Seb, treasure the moment, and bask in a happiness unlike anything he'd experienced before.

"Happy anniversary." Seb kissed him.

Anniversary. In all the New Year's Eve and gift exchange excitement, Rutger had forgotten that exactly a year had passed since Seb had arrived for a two-day visit, which had never ended.

"Happy anniversary," Rutger echoed. "Have I told you today that I love you?"

"At least four times." Seb's eyes glowed as he tightened his grip on Rutger. "And I'll never get tired of hearing it." His smile was soft and tender. "I love you too."

A bounce on the lower end of the bed announced Raeynar's arrival, and moments later, he'd snuggled up against Rutger's back.

Perfection. Rutger sighed. He would never know how he'd gotten this lucky. Somewhere someone was looking out for him and had given him everything he'd never known he needed.

Rutger stared at the man he loved. He'd thought games were his life until Seb came and showed him the only prize worth playing for was love.

About the Author

Helena Stone can't remember a life before words and reading. After growing up in a household where no holiday or festivity was complete without at least one new book, it is hardly surprising she now owns more books than shelf space while her Kindle is about to explode.

The urge to write came as a surprise. The realization that people might enjoy her words was a shock to say the least. Now that the writing bug has well and truly taken hold, Helena can no longer imagine not sharing the characters in her head and heart with the rest of the world.

Having left the hustle and bustle of Amsterdam for the peace and quiet of the Irish countryside she divides her time between reading, writing, long and often wet walks with the dog, her part-time job in a library, a grown-up daughter and her ever loving and patient husband.

Helena can be found and contacted here:
http://helenastone.blogspot.ie/

Also by Helena Stone

MM Romance (Novels)

Double Dutch Courage

Patience *(Dublin Virtues Trilogy #1)*

Equality *(Dublin Virtues Trilogy #2)*

Renewal *(Dublin Virtues Trilogy #3)*

Scenes from Adelaide Road

MM Romance (Novellas & Short Stories)

Too Hot for Santa

A Miracle in the Library (*Mitch & Cian #1*)

Lessons in Love (*Mitch & Cian #2*)

Pride of Place *(Mitch & Cian #3)*

Ukuleles & Scrums *(Mitch & Cian #4)*

The Rest of Our Lives *(Mitch & Cian #5)*

Careful What You Wish For

Valentine's Love *(Valentine's Love #1)*

Valentine's Surprise *(Valentine's Love #2)*

Valentine's Vows *(Valentine's Love #3)*

Once Upon a Gingerbread Reindeer *(A Free Read)*

The Blowhole Series

All or Nothing (MF)

Little Rainbows (MF)

Now or Never (MM)